Three Layers of Guilt

The first time he heard the scream, he automatically tried to identify it in terms of animal life—a rabbit, newly caught by a stoat—but even so he was disturbed enough to stop reading. The second scream convinced him that this was no animal.

He jumped to his feet, scattering the book on the floor, raced through the kitchen, where he picked up a torch, and out of the back door. There were several stout sticks just outside and he grabbed one. With torch switched on he raced round the corner of the house, down the short path to the gate, and out on to the concrete drive.

The third scream, more violent, came from his left. As he ran on, he heard a shout: 'Shut the silly bitch up.'

A hundred and fifty yards away a car was stopped by the verge and in the beam of his torch he saw a woman who struggled with two men. The men, keeping their faces turned away from him, roughly pushed her away so that she stumbled on to the verge. Then they jumped into the car, and drove off at speed. He tried to read the registration number, but the plate was plastered with mud and he was able to make out only AK and 32, together with the last letter K.

The woman came to her feet. Her mackintosh had been wrenched open, her cardigan buttons had been ripped off, and her white blouse had been torn. He recognized Anne O'Reilly.

Other titles in the Walker British Mystery series

Marian Babson • THE LORD MAYOR OF DEATH

John Creasey • HELP FROM THE BARON

Elizabeth Lemarchand • UNHAPPY RETURNS

W.J. Burley • DEATH IN WILLOW PATTERN

William Haggard • YESTERDAY'S ENEMY

John Sladek • INVISIBLE GREEN

Elizabeth Lemarchand • STEP IN THE DARK

Simon Harvester • ZION ROAD

John Creasey • THE TOFF AND THE FALLEN ANGELS

J.G. Jeffreys • SUICIDE MOST FOUL

Peter Alding • MURDER IS SUSPECTED

Simon Harvester • MOSCOW ROAD

JEFFREY ASHFORD
Three Layers of Guilt

WALKER AND COMPANY · NEW YORK

First published in the United States of America in 1976 by the
Walker Publishing Company, Inc.

This paperback edition first published in 1983.

ISBN: 0-8027-3016-7

Library of Congress Catalog Card Number: 75-27060

Printed in the United States of America

10   9   8   7   6   5   4   3   2   1

I

Harry Miles braked for the cross-roads, found his way was clear, and accelerated across. He passed the pub, a side lane, and then a bungalow with over-trimmed grass verge and geometrically neat flower beds.

Just past the bungalow were woods, mixed in character, and obviously not commercially valuable, then beyond a bend these gave way to a large grass field. At the far corner of the field was a clump of trees between which could be seen the roofs of two buildings. The one to the left, he thought, must be the old priory. Having a love of the past, he'd looked up the history of the priory before journeying down. Little seemed to be known about it other than that after dissolution its treasures had never been recovered and tradition had it that these were hidden in the muddy depths of the fish ponds, also that a monk, head bloody, paced the building every July the twentieth and to see him was to suffer great misfortune.

The priory gateway consisted of curving brickwork with white stone uprights, a collection of carved heraldic beasts, and huge, highly ornamental wrought-iron gates. He smiled. Only a vast castle could really do justice to those gates.

Immediately inside the gates and to the left were buildings, a combined lodge and converted stables block, built around a courtyard. A Rolls was being washed down. The drive went round in a semi-circle and just before it reached the house, split into three: one arm going to the old priory, one to the tradesmen's entrance of the new house, one to the front door. Was he expected to take the tradesmen's entrance? He smiled again as he carried on round to the front door.

From outside, the house was ugly, a mishmash of architectural quirks which time had turned into blunders. The over-large porch was ringed with crenellations and on the flat roof was a flagpole from which flew a burgee. If the Queen flew her standard over Buckingham Palace when in residence, why shouldn't Geoffrey Blaze Pattison?

The bell pull was of brass, in the shape of a bull's head. He pulled it and then turned and looked out. The circular flower bed was dug, ready for bedding-out plants and in the rockery beyond he could just make out the backside of a man who was bent double to weed. A person could live right royally on just the staff's salaries.

He heard footsteps clacking on a hard surface and the oak door was opened by a woman, in her late fifties, with a thick, chunky face that was at the same time ugly yet attractive, because of an underlying sense of cheerful compassion. ' 'Morning,' he said, 'my name's Miles. I've an appointment with Mr. Pattison.'

'Yes, of course. Do come in.' She had a soft, sweet voice, with just the hint of a lisp. 'I'm afraid Mr. Pattison's very busy at the moment, but I'm sure he'll be as quick as he can. Been working very hard recent, he has. Too hard.'

He was surprised to catch the note of genuine concern in her voice.

She led the way across the hall – very small and unimposing for such a house – into a large, oblong room.

'Do sit down and make yourself comfortable, Mr. Miles. There's some cigarettes in the box there.'

After she'd left, he helped himself to a cigarette from the heavily chased silver cigarette box, then crossed the luxuriously carpeted floor to one of the two bay windows, with leaded panes, and stared out. The ground rolled away, to drop down to the Pecton Marshes (marsh only in name since the fifteenth century). Beyond the marshes was the sea, a thin ribbon of bright blue. A large tanker was fairly close inshore. Today, tankers of half a million tons were at sea. In his day, a fifteen thousand tonner had been a big one. He brought his gaze inland. A herd of Friesians were paddock grazing in the nearest field. There were too many thistles amongst the grass: a few thistles didn't really matter, but this number spelled out sloppy farming. He noticed the barbed wire fence which had one stake rotted and leaning over and the metal gate which hung badly.

The unusual ormolu grandmother clock struck eleven and he looked across at it. He knew virtually nothing about antiques, but could be certain this clock was valuable: this was Pattison's house. The room was filled (overfilled) with lovely and valuable things: grand piano with a patina like glass, a set of Hepplewhite chairs, heavily inlaid cabinets filled with porcelain figurines, French prisoner-of-war bone models, a matching pair of escritoires, silver pheasants on marble mantelpiece, five paintings . . . Were those the famous Impressionist paintings, said in one article he'd read recently to be worth over a million pounds? A million pounds. It was an awe-inspiring thought – except it didn't fill him with awe, merely a kind of regret that such wealth should be locked up in something so unproductive.

He stubbed out one cigarette, lit another. Curiosity as much as anything had brought him to this house. Was a millionaire's gratitude lasting? What would Pattison look like after more than thirty years?

He sat down in one of the two green leather armchairs and sank deep down into comfort. Wealth might be bad for the soul, but it was great for the body.

There hadn't been much comfort that day or for the six following days. Strangely, he could remember the Friday with such clarity it was as if it had only just passed, yet the days before and the days after were only dimly recorded. He could even visualize the ragged patch of cumulous which had slowly formed itself into the shape of a running dog ...

2

The stand-by switched on the deckhead light and shook his shoulders and reluctantly he awoke, reaching up through the layers of consciousness.

'One bell, it's blowing a bloody gale, and the rain's dropping like it's another flood.'

'Thanks,' he mumbled. Thanks for what? That chapter of disasters? He heard Taggart leave the cabin. He must force himself to get up now ...

'Five to and you snoring fit to wake the old man! It's a great life for the gentry.'

He threw the bedclothes back and sat up, knowing this was the only way of forcing himself to act before he fell asleep again. Nothing had prepared him for the mind-destroying tiredness that came from double watches. At navigational school they'd taught him how to take bearings, shoot the sun, calculate the draught, stow cheese away from strong smelling items . . . But not how to overcome the drug-like effects of fours hours on watch, four hours off, when one was barely sixteen.

He dressed in a panicky hurry because he was going to be late, left the cabin. In the chartroom, the chief officer was slumped on the settee, eyes tight shut, while the second officer was writing up the log. Miles walked on. In the asdic cabin, the relief was talking to his oppo. Only a handful of merchant ships had asdic and the majority didn't know how lucky they were. It kept going wrong and giving false echoes which sent them scurrying off course. Beyond the asdic cabin was the wheelhouse, lit only by the ghostly green glow from the gyro repeater, the white glow from the steering compass, and the emergency light over the zig-zag board.

As Miles walked over to the port door, the zig-zag clock buzzed. The helmsman, his relief standing by his side, put on five degrees of port helm.

'Is that you, Fourth?' demanded the third, in an irritated voice.

'No, sir,' he answered, 'it's Miles.'

'You sound like a herd of elephants. Where the hell's the fourth?'

'I don't know, sir.' Miles hurriedly opened the port door and stepped out. He went round the blast shield out on to the wing.

Miles had accepted Taggart's description of the weather and had dressed accordingly : oilskins, sea boots, towel round his neck, and sou'wester crammed down over his head. But the sky was clear, the moon was bright, and what little sea there was was mainly a lazy swell so that the *Oakmore* pitched only slightly.

Smith, his fellow cadet, came up to him. 'What's up with you, then? Thinking of going to sea?' He chuckled.

If Miles hadn't been so dulled from sleep down in the cabin, he'd have realized from the lack of movement that the stand-by's weather report had to be nonsense.

'Shall we 'oist the mainsail?' asked one of the DEMS seamen from the oerlikon gun emplacement built up on top of the wing.

The chief officer came out of the wheelhouse. 'Shut that bloody row up. Miles, I've told you before to pipe down. Next time, I'll have you chipping and red leading until your knees are raw.' The chief officer withdrew.

'Silly bastard,' said Smith, when certain he wouldn't be heard.

'Never 'eard such a noisy bloke as you in all my born naturals,' said the DEMS rating.

'All clear, course two forty-three, error one east, and the sandwiches are stale again,' said Smith. He yawned. 'She's all yours, then. God, I'm tired!' He hurried off the wing into the wheelhouse.

Miles leaned on the for'd wooden dodger, his head just clear of the board, and fell asleep. He woke to hear the chief officer say, through one of the vision slits in the blast shield: 'Aren't you having any tea?' The chief wasn't motivated by kindness: he was checking up that the cadet hadn't fallen asleep.

'Thought I saw something,' said Miles. 'Just making certain.' Eight days, five of them in convoy, had taught him the necessity of always having a good reason for doing whatever he was doing.

He went into the wheelhouse. The tray was on one of the lockers. The tea was tepid and the sandwiches were stale. He returned to the wing and went up the ladder to the monkey island for a cigarette, only to find the fourth was already there, smoking behind cupped hands. He said he'd come to take an azimuth and the fourth cursed, crushed the cigarette out in his fingers, and left down the starboard ladder.

Miles removed the cover of the gyro repeater, swung the azimuth mirror round, and tilted the lens to bring the image of Betelgeuse down on to the compass card. That done, he brought out a pack of cigarettes and lit one.

When he took the star bearing down to the chartroom, he found the chief officer asleep, leaning against the chart table. The chief officer awoke, shut the chart to try to make out he'd been working at it, and stalked out. Miles read G.M.T. off one of the chronometers and used the tables to calculate the compass error at one east. He entered the figure in the compass log.

He returned to the wing. The bridge could be paced athwartships or fore and aft, which latter took him past the weird rocket devices, FAMs and PACs which everyone hoped would never have to be fired in anger. He paced alternatively fore and aft and athwartships. In theory, the variety of route helped him to stay awake. In practice, he went to sleep each time and awoke at the turn or, sometimes, as he crashed into the rails.

'At sea,' his father had said once, 'you'll be close to the infinite: tuned in to God.' His father often advised God as he ploughed or cultivated a field. All Miles was tuned in to was sleep.

After a time, the sky lightened to the east. Miles went into the wheelhouse and brought out a pair of glasses to check the horizon, which proved to be clear. He stared for'd at the deck cargo of crated planes, said to be Spitfires. Pilots didn't have to do double watches.

The captain arrived, only seconds after tea and hot

buttered toast, at four bells. He was in a bloody mood. His last ship had been torpedoed and, although his seamanship had got him to an island where they'd lain for four months as they patched the gaping hole with concrete and wood, he'd lost his confidence. A short, weatherbeaten, gnarled runt of a man, he stared at Miles with open hostility. 'Were you making all that row during the night?'

'No, sir.'

'I've told you all before, you're to keep quiet up here.'

'Yes, sir.'

The captain glared round the wing, hoping to find something more definite he could complain about, but failed. He withdrew.

One of the phones buzzed to send Miles scurrying into the wheelhouse: the blue light was on over the crow's nest phone. 'Look-out relieved. All clear.'

Miles went through to the starboard wing. The captain, legs firmly astride, was urinating into the drainage channel, the fourth was conscientiously keeping a watch for'd. 'Look-out's been relieved,' reported Miles, thinking that the captain had too, 'and all's clear.'

'Humph!' said the captain.

Only two hours to breakfast, breakfast relief, and then a couple of hours kip, thought Miles as he turned to re-enter the wheelhouse. He took one step forward towards the blast screen and as he moved his weight on to his left leg the torpedo struck. There was an explosion and the fourteen-thousand-ton ship shook so fiercely that he was flung against the blast screen with a force that bruised his shoulder. The captain was sent sprawling on all fours, the fourth hit the wooden dodger rail. A column of water rose up in a fan shape just abaft the funnel.

As the captain picked himself up, he began to shout orders, but only the first few words were comprehensible because a second torpedo struck them for'd, in the middle of number three hatch. This explosion flayed the bridge with spears of metal. The fourth, who'd just begun to massage his stomach, collapsed, his head split open. Miles stared down at the crumpled figure, head pouring blood and brains out to stain the white, holystoned deck and he knew a sickening, nauseated disbelief.

'Phone the engine-room and ask them for a damage report,' ordered the captain, strangely calm in the face of real danger. 'Sound the alarm.'

The ship began to list. A few things on the locker tops in the wheelhouse rolled to starboard, the door of a flag locker clanged open. Abruptly, with a noise that startled them, a gush of steam hissed out of the funnel. The chief officer ran out on to the wing as Miles ran into the wheelhouse. They collided, but neither was thrown off his feet. Miles crossed the wheelhouse to the red alarm bell, to the right of the helmsman, and pressed it: strident bells rang throughout the ship. No alarm had ever been less necessary.

'How bad is it?' demanded the helmsman, in a hoarse voice.

'I don't know,' said Miles, beginning to suffer a chest-tightening fear as the first shock wore off. 'The fourth's out there, dead.'

The zig-zag clock buzzed. Automatically, the helms-man checked the board and then put on five degrees starboard helm.

Miles picked up the telephone to the engine-room and pressed the call button. At that moment, he heard the captain order stop engines and the clang of bells as the chief officer moved the engine-room telegraph to stop.

There was no answering clang of bells. Nor was the telephone being answered. He pressed the call button for a second and longer time. The line was always alive and normally there was a continual, even roar of machinery, but to his heightened perception it seemed the note had changed. He heard a series of high pitched sounds which seemed to be screams.

The chief officer ran into the wheelhouse. 'What's the report from below?'

'I can't get any answer.'

The chief officer grabbed the phone from him and pressed the call button for a full ten seconds. The bos'n, almost as broad as he was tall, with complexion of tanned leather, wearing a polo-neck sweater over pyjama trousers, came in from the starboard wing. 'Stand by the boats,' ordered the chief officer. 'Tell Chippy to get down on the fore deck and sound the holds.'

The bos'n left and went down to the boat-deck where the lifeboats had, from the beginning of the trip, been swung out and lowered to a level with the deck, there lashed fast against fenders with canvas bands with quick release tackle.

The second and third officers arrived from below at the same moment. They each carried a panic bag: they were men who took great care of themselves.

The chief wireless officer, an effeminate man, hurried into the wheelhouse in the wake of the other two officers. His face was twisted with fear. 'How bad are we hit?' he demanded shrilly.

'We've sunk,' replied the second. 'Can't you see the fish through the ports?'

The three of them went out on to the wing. Almost immediately, the chief wireless officer and the second officer returned to go into the chartroom to work out their position and transmit it in an S.O.S.

Miles called the engine-room once more. This time, he could be certain he heard screaming. He held the receiver away from his ears, but the screams pursued him. Then he heard a voice. He spoke.

'Bridge. The captain wants to know what the damage is.'

The third officer came into the wheelhouse and grabbed the receiver from Miles. 'Third here . . . Yeah . . . Have you stopped engines . . . For Christ's sake, man, you've got to . . . I don't know.' He slammed the receiver back on its hook. 'They can't stop the engines.' He turned and ran out to the wing.

The list was increasing, a fact brought home by the constant noise of articles moving. Miles went for'd and stared out through a port. Coming up from the west was a cloud of cumulous which was taking on the appearance of a running dog, with outstretched head.

Smith arrived on the bridge, as always late. 'And I bought a whole load of new kit before sailing,' he moaned. 'I could've boozed the money instead.' He was large, solid, seventeen, without imagination and seemingly wholly without fear. Miles had never envied anyone so much.

The engine-room phone buzzed. Someone, never accurately identified, reported that the engines had at last been stopped, that the water was rising so fast the engine-room must be abandoned, the electrical supply could not last more than a few more moments, three greasers were dead, the second and fifth engineers were dead, four men were gravely injured.

Miles reported to the captain. The captain grunted. He looked aft, at the funnel from which oily black smoke and white superheated steam were gushing, then walked to the after rails. He shouted to the bos'n to detail six men to go down to the engine-room to give a hand getting up the injured. His manner, in sharp contrast to what it had been before the torpedoing, was calmly confident.

The chief officer, just returned from the fore-deck, reported. Number three hold was making water fast: number two was still dry.

The captain looked at his wrist watch. 'Seven thirty-three,' he said. He shifted his weight as the list increased. 'Well, Chief, she's going to go. Get below and call the port boat crews over to starboard : we're not going to be able to lower the port boats. Have hands standing by what rafts can be launched and they're to launch on orders from the bridge.' He studied the officers and cadets. 'The rest of you get our position and the course to the nearest land and then take up boat stations . . . Good luck.'

Miles followed Smith into the chartroom and they waited whilst the second officer used parallel rulers to take off their course, having in mind the prevailing trades. Miles could see the small pencil cross that marked their morning star position. On the chart, land was only inches away.

Events suddenly crowded each other. There was a sharp, vibrating noise from somewhere below, which the third nervously identified as a bulkhead going, then the list abruptly increased. They hurried off the bridge and made their way through the press of crew to their boats : in Miles's case, his new boat, since previously he'd been detailed to the port midships one.

Two A.B.s were seated at each of the crucifixes, ready to cast off some of the turns of the falls and lower. Two O.S.s were standing by the quick release shackles. The remainder of the swollen crew stood back by the bulkhead of the radio cabin and among them were four passengers.

There was a swirl amongst the men to Miles's right and he looked aft. Two badly injured men from the engine-room – in singlets and cotton trousers – were being carefully lowered on to the deck. One of them screamed with agony as the improvised stretcher was lowered: his face was the colour of boiled lobster and his eyes had disappeared beneath puckered flesh. God, thought Miles, how much agony did a man have to suffer before he was allowed to die?

The order to abandon ship was given. The officer in charge of each boat sent men into the boats. Quick release shackles were sprung, canvas lashings released, and the boats swung out with lurching movements. Men hung on to the grab lines, made fast to wires between the davits, but relaxed their holds when the boats settled down to pick up the easy rhythm of the ship which was rolling slightly to the swell.

'Lower away.'

The A.B.s released the turns of the falls until only one and a half criss-crosses remained on the crucifixes. They lowered, letting the ropes slide over the smooth metal.

Miles's boat was first down. From above, the swell had looked slight, but when they were just above the sea it rose up regularly with the menacing ease of uncontrollable strength.

The third officer might be a slob of a man, but he was a good seaman. He stopped the lowering as a swell dropped, gave the order to resume lowering as the swell was about to reach its trough, and judged events perfectly so that the boat was caught and lifted by the next uprising swell to take the weight off the falls. The seamen fore and aft unhooked the blocks When that swell dropped away, the boat was riding free.

The leading lifeboat was not so skilfully handled. The after fall was released, but the weight never came properly off the for'd fall and the seamen couldn't release the block. When the swell dipped away, the boat upended. Men tumbled out in a wild jumble of arms and legs: the hideously burned greaser plummeted into the sea and vanished: an O.S. who'd grabbed at the falls had his hand jammed in the block and he hung, with all his weight coming on his shattered fingers.

One man, small, skinny, with a mop of bright ginger hair, was thrown well clear, but for some reason he wasn't wearing a life-jacket. When he surfaced, he threshed wildly with his hands, churning the water into foam before he sank.

Miles never knew what prompted him to stand up on the thwart and then go over the side: with all the deaths there had been already, with all the deaths there must inevitably be to come, one unknown man's death was really of no account.

The water was oily, because some of the ship's double bottoms had crumpled, and he remembered that fuel oil burned lungs and stomach so he swam with a modified breast stroke which pushed aside the surface of the water as he moved.

He caught a quick glimpse of ginger hair, just below the surface. He'd never been taught life saving, so he grabbed the hair and pulled and a face broke surface. The man gasped, vomited, and began to struggle so violently that Miles was about to let go of him when a boat hook caught hold of his coat and he was towed in to the boat and pulled up over the gunwale. Miles reached the boat in a few strokes and two seamen helped him inboard. Water poured off him and he began to shiver as the wind, feeling keen despite the sunshine, cut into his flesh.

'Take your clothes off and wring them out,' advised the third, before giving orders to give way together. In some disorder they lowered their oars into the rollocks and pulled.

They were some hundred yards away when the *Oakmore* began to sink much more rapidly. She went down by the head until the water was over the fo'c's'le, her twin screws surfaced, there was a crescendo of noise as everything possible broke free, she hung there for a time, then she went straight down with heartbreaking speed.

The captain appeared not to have been saved. The chief officer gave orders for the second lifeboat to join him in going back to search the area for survivors or useful flotsam and then to close the rafts and strip them of food and water.

The lifeboats drifted through the oily, debris-littered sea. There were several black-faced men in the water, but none seemed to be alive.

* * * * *

Out of the thirty-three men who escaped in the two boats, twenty-one survived to be picked up by a corvette, one of the outlying escorts of a large convoy. They were landed in Liverpool, given third-class railway warrants to their home towns, and told they could claim for uniforms and other equipment lost but that it was unlikely their claims would be met in full. After all, there was a war on.

Three months later, when in Sydney, Miles received a letter from Pattison which had been forwarded by the shipping company. Pattison wanted to thank Miles for saving his life, hoped that at the first opportunity Miles would come and see him so that he could thank him more personally, and promised all possible help should it ever be needed.

3

Geoffrey Pattison had been newsworthy for many years, typifying as he did the ever-popular rags-to-riches saga. He'd been born to two missionaries who were too pious to attend to their own financial state and when they died, of some obscure tropical disease, they left him as their sole inheritance five bibles, some faded and yellowing photos of people he never definitely identified, a collection of pressed flowers, and a keen and enquiring mind that had been largely shaped by his mother's unusual form of teaching.

His passage home by ship, steerage, was paid for by a collection raised by English residents, scared that otherwise he might become a permanent charge on them. Back in England, he lived in Birmingham with his aunt and uncle and their two daughters, none of whom liked him. At first he did badly at school, because of his mother's unorthodox teaching. The headmaster called him lazy, his uncle beat him, and his two cousins told everyone that he smelled like a fuzzy-wuzzy.

Most boys would have dumbly bowed down before such a wall of misunderstanding and dislike, but he fought back, with a dedicated tenacity that at first went unremarked, and he developed a burning passion to succeed. He spent all his spare time studying his school books and making up for all his lost years, yet with a cunning that had to come from his contact with the natives in far off Africa for he gave no sign of his extended knowledge until the end-of-term exams when he wrote out all he knew with the object of surprising and confounding the school staff.

Pattison's exam papers were passed to the headmaster for his considered opinion. The headmaster was a feet-on-the-ground man and he came to the conclusion that Pattison had somehow learned what the questions were going to be and had mugged up the answers. He was a cheat and a liar. So the headmaster thrashed Pattison. As, despite himself, the tears of pain trickled down his cheeks, Pattison silently swore that never again would he give anyone the chance of beating him, either physically or metaphorically.

He left school and his uncle said he'd have to get a job and keep himself. He saw in a paper an advertisement for a clerk in a commodity broker's office and he applied for it. Forty-three other school leavers also applied for it, but he was accepted because the senior partner caught a hint of the passion to succeed which lay inside the mind of the red-headed, slightly built, open-faced, strikingly blue-eyed youth.

He lived in a crumby bed-sitter, owned one suit which he regularly darned, and dreamt of being the biggest commodity broker in the market. He studied with the eagerness of a miser pursuing gold, never spent any money except on necessaries, and was highly unpopular.

He saved the firm a great deal of money in 1934, when the great Brazilian coffee scandal broke. Working late into the night, every night, he pieced together information generally known and confidential information supplied by the firm's local agents and came to the conclusion that an immense fraud was being planned. He wrote a two-thousand-word report, advising against entering into any further coffee futures despite the apparently highly advantageous trading conditions. Two of the junior partners said he was writing nonsense and should stick to doing what he was paid to do. The senior partner disagreed and accepted the advice. Four months later other partnerships were counting their losses in tens of thousands and his firm had hardly lost a penny. A year after that, Pattison was made a junior partner.

By the outbreak of war he was senior partner and the firm now handled metals and rubber as well as sugar, coffee, and cocoa. It was generally agreed in the markets that he was the most successful man in the business and the most dislikable.

He viewed the war solely in terms of how it would affect his prosperity. His crystal-gazing left him depressed. But then the bombing got under way and he began to buy up bombed buildings and undervalued shares at bargain prices and his depression lightened.

The country demanded he register for service. In his opinion – and he had a remarkably keen appreciation of the situation – he was unlikely actually to be called up to serve in the forces, but he took the precaution of paying a specialist a hundred guineas in cash to certify he had a weak heart following childhood rheumatic fever.

The country then wanted him to help in his capacity as a businessman, asking him to go to the States and take part in negotiations for arms and food so desperately needed. He was delighted to agree to go. As a very keen businessman, he expected to make a handsome profit for himself.

But on the eighth day, the T.S.S. *Oakmore* was torpedoed and sunk.

    •   •   •   •   •

Miles heard a door click open at the far end of the long sitting-room and he half turned to face it. When he saw Pattison enter, he stood up.

'I'm so sorry to have kept you waiting all this time, Mr. Miles. Business. Business. Well, this is a very great pleasure!' Pattison came across, limping slightly.

Miles shook hands, careful not to use too strong a grip. Pattison was quite a bit smaller than Miles remembered and a lot older looking than he should be. His red hair had darkened considerably and he was fast balding. His beaky nose was even more prominent in life than in photographs.

Pattison sat down in the second arm-chair. 'Now, before anything else, what can I offer you to drink?'

'I'd like some coffee, please.'

'Do sit down. And have another cigarette.' Pattison reached over to a telephone, lifted the receiver, pressed one of the call buttons, and spoke to say he wanted coffee for both of them.

He replaced the receiver, then lifted up his right leg with both hands and placed it over his left. He smiled, to show that several of his teeth were gold-backed. 'How many years is it since we last met? Thirty-two? And all that time you've denied me the pleasure of thanking you personally. You know, I was quite hurt that you wouldn't accept my invitation to come and see me.'

'I'd have liked to, but . . .'

'But you were too embarrassed. Of course – I understand.'

23

Miles had not been going to say that.

'I suppose you're a captain now? Are you in command of one of those leviathans which give the insurance people so many sleepless nights?'

'No. I quit the sea quite soon after the war.'

'Indeed! Now what made you do that?' Pattison sounded interested, yet the set stare of his blue eyes suggested this was only from a sense of duty.

'I was going to get married and my wife didn't like me being away at sea for so long, so often.'

'Yes, of course. But tell me, why didn't you bring your wife here today so that I could meet her?'

'She died a few years ago,' replied Miles, in an expressionless voice.

'I'm so sorry to hear that. So sorry. How very sad for you. Do you have any children?'

'No, we had no children.'

Pattison lifted up his right leg and moved it off his left one. 'Ten years ago, the doctors gave me six months to live, but apart from a weak leg I'm still proving them to be fools.' He spoke with a trace of triumph.

Vera, the woman who'd let Miles into the house, entered the room with a large, clover-shaped silver tray on which were matched silver coffee and milk jugs, silver sugar bowl, and two delicately patterned cups and saucers. She offered the tray to Miles who helped himself.

When Vera offered him the tray, Pattison said : 'Vera, Mr. Miles saved my life during the war.'

'You don't say!' she exclaimed. She turned her head and looked at Miles.

'Our ship was torpedoed and then the lifeboat I was in was upended and I was tossed into the sea. I never could swim.' He chuckled briefly. 'Never had the time to learn. So I was about to go under for the last time when Mr. Miles grabbed me by my hair – I had a lot more in those days than I do now – and dragged me back up to the surface.'

'What a wonderful thing to do.'

Miles felt vaguely uncomfortable because of the depth of respect in her voice.

Pattison finished serving himself and Vera stood upright. 'I don't know if Mr. Miles will be staying to lunch . . . ?'

Miles shook his head. 'That's very kind of you, but I have to get back.'

'A very great pity. I was looking forward to a much longer stay. Still, there'll be other times.' He did not sound so disappointed as his words suggested.

'I'll put the tray down on this table,' said Vera, 'and you can help yourself to more coffee when you want.' She set the tray down and left.

Pattison rested his elbows on the arms of the chair and joined his fingertips together. 'Your letter mentioned the fact you might be glad of a little help. You have only to ask. As I wrote all those years ago when I thanked you for saving my life, I have always held myself ready to repay just a little of the tremendous debt I owe you.'

It was a pity, thought Miles, that Pattison couldn't melt off some of the sugar from his words. 'I'm sorry to bother you . . .'

'And I'm delighted you have done. Now, how can I help?'

.   .   .   .   .   .

Sylvia had had rigid standards in life which at first sight had seemed devoid of all logic. The merchant navy was not nice, farming was nice. Only later did Miles discover that her idea of farming was five hundred acres, run by a farm manager. At twenty-four, love was a nice, thick blindfold. His father had, one evening, tried to tear off the blindfold in typically blunt manner. 'Your Sylvia,' he said, as they sat in the kitchen and drank instant coffee from chipped and faded Coronation mugs, 'don't like muck.'

'Give over,' said Rachel Miles.

He ignored his wife. 'Farming's muck and nothing can't change it.'

Miles tried to keep his voice even. 'Dad, she's all right. It's just she doesn't like the way we talk about some things.'

'And small wonder at that,' said Rachel. 'Last time she was here, father couldn't talk about anything 'cept the way the A.I. milk the bulls.'

His father finished his coffee. His face was ruddy and he looked the picture of health: no one would have guessed he would be dead within three years. 'If a bloke's farming,' he said unrepentantly, 'his missus needs to know what happens. Someone's got to get the semen from the bulls.'

'Maybe, but there's ways of telling and you used the wrong way.'

'Muck's muck, however you call it.' He turned and stared at his son. 'I'm telling you straight, Harry, Sylvia's not the one for muck.'

Cold Comfort Farm, thought Miles resentfully.

'But you won't listen, I'll be bound. You always was stubborn.'

'Not half as stubborn as you,' said Rachel. 'Talking like that when your only son comes and tells you he's getting engaged. The idea of it! How'd you have liked it if

26

your father had said things to you when you told him you was marrying me?'

'How d'you know he didn't?' He grinned.

Rachel muttered something indignantly but the subject was dropped.

Miles had married Sylvia and then searched for a farm. Back in those days, there'd not only been many more farms to let, but both the experience and capital needed to get started had been very much less. He'd found a fifty-three acre farm at two pounds an acre and had bought five Channel Island cows, three hundred pullets, four breeding sows, a Fordson tractor without hydraulics, and a few essential implements, and still had some money left from what he'd saved when at sea.

Coming from a long line of farming stock, it was not really surprising that he loved farming and seldom missed the sea. He enjoyed hard work and, having a vivid imagination, he could look beyond his present small rented farm to the much larger farm he would one day own. He went to night school and learned electric arc welding and diesel engine maintenance, built a side-by-side milking parlour and installed all the equipment without help.

Because he was so busy, he couldn't take Sylvia to dances and she loved dancing. She also loved new clothes and he never gave her the money to buy them. She felt ashamed to drive around in their pre-war Austin 7, whose body had originally been two tones of brown but was now one tone of rust. And when he suggested she learned to milk in case he fell ill, she told him she wasn't going near any stinking cows ..

Because he was a romantic (although also highly practical by nature) it took him a long time to accept the truth – Sylvia was a bitch. When he did accept the

27

fact, he forced himself to come to terms with the consequences. So marriage wasn't the happy-ever-after state that he'd believed it when at the altar rails – he must just make the best of a bad job. His sense of humour and his dedication to making a success of farming helped him.

Farming entered the age of specialization, increasing size of unit, and heavy capitalization, and there was less and less room for the small, general, one-man farm. As their living standards went down, through no fault of his, Sylvia's bitching increased.

The tide of specialization grew stronger, egged on by governments who declared their proud love for their yeoman farmers and then made certain these same yeoman farmers were put to the wall. He took the only reasonable course left to him and cut out all livestock other than cows, expanded the herd as far as he was able, and worked seven days a week, fifty-two weeks a year. He made less and less money, the harder he worked.

Sylvia became friendly with a man called Timothy, a successful car salesman, smoothly handsome, and very self-confident. He loved dancing, went abroad every year, and was contemptuously amused that anyone could be stupid enough to work on a farm and earn nothing. He used to ask Sylvia and Miles to dances, knowing full well that Miles must refuse. Sylvia accepted. Miles, who knew a loyalty that was very old-fashioned, suspected nothing until she came home very late one night and couldn't quite hide her guilty apprehension. He normally managed to control his temper, but that night he didn't and she was so frightened she promised to turn over a whole new chapter and never again meet or go out with Timothy.

She continued seeing Timothy, but for a time he didn't

know this because she persuaded a friend, Madge, to cover up for her. His moment of truth came when he learned that she and Timothy had been in a car crash in which both of them had died.

He continued to farm, showing a dogged perseverance that one or two people were stupid enough to call positively bovine. Then the owner of the farm applied for, and obtained, planning permission for most of the land. There was monetary compensation for Miles, but no money could compensate him for all that he'd put into that soil.

He sold up and went to the Mediterranean to find sun, warm sea, and forgetfulness. He had no plans, no itinerary, no objective. When he liked a place he stayed there, when he got fed up he moved on. From time to time he worked: he crewed a rich man's yacht in Menton and wondered at the strange things wealth did, cultivated chrysanthemums in Ventimiglia, became a waiter in Cagliari. Sometimes he was on his own, sometimes he lived with a woman, enjoying a loving passion that Sylvia had denied him. A rich divorcee in Monte Carlo begged him to marry her: a long-legged blonde in Torremolinos theatrically threatened to commit suicide if he left her (when, perturbed, he made enquiries about her fate a few days later, he learned she'd become very friendly with a husky Swede).

After his money was gone, but for two hundred pounds, he decided to return to England. He regretted nothing. Success was interesting, but it certainly wasn't worth mortgaging one's life for it. He might own virtually nothing, but he had learned that life needed to be viewed with ironic detachment.

He'd get a job (enough of the English character remained in him to make him wary of becoming a full-time beachcomber), but one day he'd return to the sun and the gentle spirit of mañana.

.   .   .   .   .

'So,' said Pattison, who'd been briefly told part of the story, 'you wondered if I could help you get a job?'

'That's right,' agreed Miles.

'I shall certainly do all I possibly can.'

Nicely qualified, under the guise of wide, open-hearted, generous assistance, decided Miles. But then no rich man had ever become rich through generosity of character. And having been in Pattison's company now for half an hour, or so, he'd been able to catch echoes of the harsh, fanatical desire to stay successful and rich which lay beneath that fulsome manner.

Pattison brought a pigskin cigar case from his pocket. He offered it – Miles refused – then took a cigar and carefully cut the end. 'I take it you want to return to farming?'

'Yes, I do. I'm really looking for a job as farm manager.'

Pattison lit the cigar with a Swan Vesta match. He drew on it appreciatively. 'From all you've told me, I gather you never went to any agricultural college?'

'No, I didn't. But I can show farming ancestry and twenty years' practical experience.'

'These days, though, the techniques have become so scientific . . .' He let his voice trail away. He was not going to be sufficiently ill-mannered to point out Miles's deficiencies more specifically.

Miles smiled. 'Some men get weighed down with scientific and agricultural degrees and have difficulty in making anything grow, others are so ignorant they can

30

make a stone grow and not know why. I'm one of the latter. I reckon I'm the better bet.'

'I admire a man with plenty of self-confidence,' said Pattison, a trace of annoyance in his voice. 'I'll tell you what I'll do. I'll speak to various friends and acquaintances and see what they suggest. How will that be?'

'Fine. And thanks.'

Pattison momentarily frowned, as if he had expected far more fulsome gratitude than he'd received. 'Then if you'll leave me an address to which I can have a letter sent?'

'I'll write it out now.' Miles did so, using the back of an old envelope. He handed it over.

'Good, good. Let's hope we find exactly what you want.' He put the envelope down on a small table.

Relieved he could discharge a debt at so little cost to himself? wondered Miles, certain in his own mind that Pattison had already mentally dictated a letter of polite regrets at having been unable to find any suitable position.

4

The letter from Pattison arrived twelve days later. Every effort had been made, ran the typewritten letter, to help Mr. Miles in finding the kind of job he wanted, but unfortunately without success. Employers these days wanted farm managers who had been specifically trained in all the modern, scientific advances: regretfully, it had to be admitted that a natural ability was no longer enough. However, if a cheque would be of the slightest use . . . ?

Miles thanked Mr. Pattison for all his help and declined the cheque.

A month later Miles took a job as an assistant cowman. He didn't like it. He needed to do a job to the best of his ability and this farm was farmed by clock-watchers because the owners were a limited company whose only interest in soil and animals was return on capital and capital appreciation. After a few weeks, he remembered the rich divorcee in Monte Carlo and the long-legged blonde in Torremolinos with a deep nostalgia.

One Sunday, when the light was even greyer, the clouds lower, the drizzle drizzlier than before, Miles was reading the *Sunday Express* in the sitting-room of his two bedroomed house when he came across an article on Pattison. Much of it was a rehash of what he'd read before. The strange, poor, lonely childhood, the fierce battle to succeed, the incredibly keen mind and the ability to sense a market trend before anyone else, the character mixture of hard business ruthlessness and kind benevolence, the gifts to charity, the prison visiting from a declared sense of involvement in human disaster, the dramatic war-time episode when his ship had been torpedoed and he'd only just escaped drowning, the post-war career in property development, the small but justly famous collection of Impressionist paintings bought before prices of these had skyrocketed, the collection of antique gold frogs from Peru, and the other treasures which filled the mansion he lived in. The writer then went on (and it was clear he had not liked Pattison one little bit) to mention briefly the latest, and by far the largest of Pattison's property deals which to date, and uncharacteristically, was not proving successful. But, finished the writer, with a man like Pattison success was often made to rise out of failure, like an orchid growing out of a pile of rotting manure.

Miles smiled – did orchids grow in manure?

. . . . .

The head cowman was a morose individual with an obsession for tidiness. Miles was amused that any man could find life so tedious because of such piffling details and unfortunately he did not hide his amusement too well. This led to their row over the milk scoop. The head cowman ordained that when not in use the scoop must be on its peg, on the wall, above the wash tank. In a hurry to go round to one of the yards to give a hand where, to judge from the bellowings of a bullock, it was needed, Miles left the scoop on the edge of the bulk tank. The head cowman saw it there and moaned and when Miles shrugged his shoulders he became furious and said that Miles had better find a job somewhere else.

. . . . .

Miles returned to his cousin's house in Northamptonshire and asked if he could stay there until he found himself a new job. His cousin said she'd be delighted to put him up for as long as he wanted, but why didn't he just return to all the sun he was always talking so longingly about? He tried to explain that he'd only go back when he'd saved enough money to prevent the necessity of his becoming the beachcomber he wanted to become, but she laughed and said she didn't understand a word.

Miles replied to advertisements in the weekly farming magazines and arranged to go for an interview to a farm in Oxford on the Wednesday. That morning there was a letter for him. It was from Breakthorn Priory and signed A. Simon, Land agent. The position of farm manager on the home farm had just fallen vacant and Mr. Miles might like to be interviewed for that job by the writer. Would he arrive on either Monday or Tuesday next, with an itemized and, if possible, receipted account of his expenses for the journey, which same would be reimbursed.

    •   •   s   •   g

Ardscastle station had been rebuilt when the line was electrified and now the booking office, offices, and a newsagent, were in a small complex built over the six tracks. Miles handed in his half of the ticket, went down the split flight of stairs to street level. There were five waiting taxis and the first one drove him out to Breakthorn Priory.

The day was windy and cold. He crossed to the pretentious, crenellated porch and snuggled deeper into his short length duffle coat. It was the kind of wind to chill a cow to her bones and drop her milk yield. Did townspeople realize that a sharp wind could appreciably cut a farmer's income? He pulled the bull's head and heard the discreet door chimes sound inside. Soon, Vera opened the door and she immediately recognized him. 'Hullo, Mr. Miles. Like the North Pole today, isn't it? Come on inside where it's warm.'

Chatting thirteen to the dozen, she led the way left out of the hall and down a corridor, stopped at the first door on the left, knocked, and opened the door. 'Mr. Simon's waiting inside,' she said.

Miles instinctively disliked Simon on sight and it was not a decision he had later ever to reconsider. Simon was tall and thin, with a pear-shaped, heavily lined face. He had a tooth-brush moustache, tinged with grey, which he was constantly brushing with crooked forefinger, a hail-fellow-well-met-but-I'm-the-boss voice, and he wore the kind of clothes that deliberately suggested a retired officer: crested blazer, striped tie (regimental?), coloured shirt, baggy grey flannels, and expensive brogues.

'Ah! good morning, Miles. Glad you got here safely.' He gestured with his right hand. 'Do sit down.'

Miles sat down on the uncomfortable wooden chair. The room was painted in two shades of institutional brown and was furnished as an office with table, desk, two filing cabinets, an old-fashioned safe, and several shelves which were filled with text-book-looking books. On the plain wooden table were several neatly arranged folders and on the long wall opposite the single window was a large scale map of the area, with the estate picked out with red boundaries.

Simon seemed to become annoyed by Miles's self-composure. 'You received my letter so you know the general situation,' he said, a touch of aggressiveness in his voice.

Miles nodded.

'As I stated in that letter, Mr. Pattison has – very generously, in my estimation – considered you for the position of farm manager.' He picked up, with precise movements, one of the folders and placed it exactly in front of himself, opened it, and took out four sheets of foolscap: these he fidgeted precisely square. 'I note that you have no previous experience in the position of farm manager?'

'I haven't any, no, but I farmed on my own for a number of years.'

'I wouldn't call that the same thing at all.'

He'd love to find good reason to deny him the job, thought Miles. But he must have had his orders. Which was strange, because Pattison had seemed so surely a man not given to helping others unless he profitted by it . . .

'This farm is primarily a dairy farm. The very large herd of Friesians is naturally accredited and . . .'

Miles only half listened. After only briefly seeing the place from the road or the house, he was quite certain he knew more about the real conditions than Simon did. It was in a bad state, probably because the previous farm manager had been slack.

Simon produced his handkerchief from his coat sleeve, blew his nose, then brushed his moustache. 'You do understand, do you, that it is a very responsible job?'

'Of course.'

Simon frowned. 'You are very self-confident,' he snapped.

'Wouldn't you think that a good thing?'

Simon brushed his moustache yet again. 'Your own farm was only fifty acres, this one is over five hundred. Do you feel you can run it as it has been run?'

'As well, or better, depending on how exactly I find things and if I can have all the equipment that I need.'

'You'll find all the necessary equipment here and the other staff are first class.'

'Then everything will be O.K.'

Simon was more plainly disgruntled. 'Very well, then, Mr. Miles. In accordance with Mr. Pattison's wishes, you will be engaged as farm manager. You'll be paid a flat rate of thirty-eight pounds a week and will be expected to work whatever hours the job requires.'

'That's a bit low for this big a job,' said Miles quietly.

'In view of your lack of experience, that's a very fair wage,' snapped Simon. 'Should you for any reason move from here, you will be much more likely to gain another job in the same position.'

36

Miles, to some extent, accepted the fact that he would be buying his experience.

'When can you start?'

'Within the week – say Thursday or Friday.'

'Thursday. Very well, that's all except to have your expenses.'

Miles gave him the list of expenses and Simon said they'd be added to his first week's wage packet. Then, after the curtest of good-byes, Simon replaced the papers in the folder, opened another folder, and began to work.

Miles left and as he closed the door, Vera came along the corridor. 'How did it go then? With his lordship?' She jerked her head scornfully in the direction of the office. 'Did he say yes?'

'He did, and I'm starting on Thursday.'

'That's wonderful, that really is! I was so hoping . . . but him!' She jerked her head again. 'You never know with him. You're going to like it here.'

'I'm sure I shall,' he answered. 'I wonder if I can telephone now for a taxi to take me to the station?'

'There's no call for that. Mr. Pattison's in London for a few days so Max can drive you later, but you'll need some grub. How about a meal with me and cook?'

He was feeling hungry and said so. 'Come on, then, and I'll tell cook there's an extra. She may make a bit of a moan, but don't take no notice, she doesn't mean it. Ever since the Spanish bloke's been here, asking for all sorts of queer things . . . Octopus. Imagine eating octopus!'

'What's he doing here?'

'Miguel's cleaning up them paintings what are said to be worth so much it makes me scared just to look at 'em. Talk about taking his time! I could clean 'em all in a morning, that's fact.'

Miles had a wonderful mental image of Vera's cleaning the paintings with soap and water.

She led the way into the very large and luxuriously equipped kitchen where the cook, middle-aged and with the features of a constant worrier, was mixing something in a large bowl on the central formica-topped table.

'Mr. Miles is coming to work on Thursday,' said Vera, 'and he's having lunch with us afore he returns home.'

The cook sighed.

'I was telling him about Miguel Luque,' went on Vera.

'Him!' The cook finished mixing and stood up, easing her back. 'It's a wonder he's still alive, seeing what he eats.'

Later, the cook offered Miles a sherry and then poured him out a large glassful of El Cid. A millionaire's staff might not be paid very well, he thought, but they nevertheless managed to live well.

5

Just over five hundred acres all told, which included about fifty acres in five small woods. Breakthorn Priory Home Farm contained both clay and loam, with the dividing line very sharply defined. The land around the farm buildings was down to permanent pastures and that further afield to regularly rotated lays or corn. The farm had deteriorated even more than Miles had imagined. Years of neglect had left the soil starved of goodness and essential trace elements, badly drained, and yielding only a proportion of its true potential. Fences were almost all in a state of disrepair, ditches were silted up to leave the water banked up in the fields, hedges had grown out, the trees in the edges of the woods had been allowed to poach over and impoverish many feet of land. The slurry pit had not been emptied for a very long time, no dung had recently been carried and much or its value had been leached away. No regular maintenance had been carried out on the tractors and they were caked with filth: machinery, broken but repairable, had been left out at the back of the silage and stack yards and was badly rusted.

Once satisfied he had seen and gauged the worst, Miles drew up a list of priorities and at the head of this list he placed the need to alter the slap-happy attitude of the five men who worked on the farm. He'd known this was not going to be easy, but had not expected it to be quite so difficult as he soon discovered it to be. They resented him, with a degree of bitterness he couldn't understand. They challenged his authority as far as they dared and they showed towards him a degree of personal unfriendliness that wasn't explainable solely on the grounds of their being forced to work properly once more.

. . . . .

Miles stared up at Armstrong, who sat on the M.F. 135 tractor. 'It'll help, Sid, if next time you use less revs. It'll save fuel and gateposts.'

Armstrong looked down at him. 'I'm telling you, there's something wrong with the steering of this old heap.'

'And I'm telling you, you hit that gatepost because you were going too fast.'

'I've a good mind to . . .' He stopped.

'Why not try it, whatever it is?'

Armstrong again looked quickly at Miles, then away. There was a smooth toughness about the considerably older man which made Armstrong reluctant to go too far, either verbally or physically.

Miles took a pack of cigarettes from his pocket. 'Get down and have a drag.'

Armstrong shook his head.

'Don't be so daft, man. Get down.'

Reluctantly, Armstrong pulled out the choke to stop the engine, then climbed down from the tractor. He accepted a cigarette. The sunlight picked out the lines of weakness about his mouth.

Miles struck a match for both of them. When he'd lit his cigarette, he said: 'I've been wanting a talk and now's as good as any time. What's eating everyone?'

'Nothing,' replied Armstrong sullenly. Then he said: 'All right, it's Bert. Why'd he get the sack?'

'Bert Ford, the last farm manager? I'd say that, among other things, it was because there were more thistles than weed grass and more weed grass than fine grass in the paddocks, the cows were solid with mastitis and so many of them were barren it was more like a beef herd.'

'The place was no different than it'd been for years. The guv'nor's not bothered.'

'Someone got bothered.'

'And for why? Maybe Bert had to be sacked to be able to give you the job.'

'Why d'you say that?'

'There's a story that you once saved the guv'nor's life and he promised to help you any time.'

Miles nodded. 'That's right.' He'd never told the men this.

'Then it's obvious.'

'Only if you're seeing crooked. When I came some time back to ask his help in finding a job he said he'd try, but he certainly couldn't do anything directly. If he'd wanted to kick Bert out to make room for me, he'd have done it then, but he didn't. He said he couldn't help so I went off and got another job. I was only offered this one weeks later and I reckon I was only offered it because Bert finally let things slide too far.'

Armstrong said sneeringly: 'No one would have cared how bad things got if you hadn't been around.'

'I wouldn't step over any man like you're suggesting – that's not my way of doing things.'

Armstrong dropped the cigarette and pushed it into the mud with the toe of his boot. 'You keep your opinion and I'll keep mine.' He climbed on to the tractor, started the engine which clattered into life, increased the revs with deliberate malice, engaged fourth high and left, the rear wheels kicking out chunks of mud from their heavy V treads.

So that was the trouble, thought Miles. He walked over to the post and rail fencing to lean his arms on the top rail. He stared across the fields and the road to the large circle of trees which marked the priory. It was strange that any man as clever as Pattison could have been content to see his farmland deteriorate as far as it had.

He looked up at the sky. If it had been a little colder, he'd have thought the dirty, grey clouds held the promise of snow. January and February were two months he'd always hated. They were dead months. Nothing was growing, the ground got wetter and wetter, the mud thicker and thicker, the cows became thoroughly dissatisfied and gave less and less milk, the remaining quantities of hay and silage began to shrink alarmingly quickly . . .

If this farm had been his, and not the tax-deductible plaything of a rich man, he'd never have let it get into its present state. No one with any love of land would. And without such a love, why buy land?

'Hullo. Or shouldn't I interrupt such deep concentration?'

Startled, because the mud on the concrete roadway had masked any sounds of footsteps, he swung round to face a woman he at first failed to identify, then realized must be the new secretary, Mrs. O'Reilly, who'd recently started working for Pattison. 'A bit of ripe crackling,' Armstrong had said to Fenton, in Miles's hearing. 'Warms a bloke up just to look at her, even if she is getting on.' She immediately reminded Miles of the rich divorcee in Monte Carlo. She had the same round face with too much character in it ever to be termed beautiful, the same curly black hair, the same sharp blue eyes, the same snub nose. But at a guess she was ten years older, certainly she was a shade plumper, and her clothes were practical, not extravagantly striking.

'You must be Harry Miles,' she said, in a low, pleasant voice, which contained a hint of something he couldn't immediately identify. 'What's got you so deep in thought, or is that a tactless question?'

He lied easily. 'Tact doesn't come into it. I've a problem. How to squeeze another two-acre paddock into a twenty-acre field when there isn't room for it.'

'Well, to a simple towns-person like myself, that's impossible.'

He decided that that something in her voice was challenge. 'Don't you know the maxim of us country bumpkins? "We do everything, the impossible merely takes a little longer." '

42

'I seem to have heard that before, in a slightly different context.'

'Naturally it's not original. We country bumpkins are quite incapable of originality.'

She spoke teasingly. 'I seem to have touched a sore spot?'

'It's not painful.'

She laughed, her head tilted slightly and her mouth wide, showing even teeth. 'Now what are you calling me under your breath?'

He wondered why there was this sense of challenge behind her words?

She looked down at the one gallon milk-can she had in her right hand. 'They need more milk up at the house and as I was going for a walk I said I'd risk your wrath and ask for it.'

'My wrath?'

'Vera says you guard the milk like a dragon guards its young. To get any extra beyond the daily ration is a feat.'

'Which you volunteered to attempt.'

'I'm not scared of dragons.'

'Come on, then, even if it ruins my fiery reputation.' He took the milk-can from her.

They walked along the concrete drive, past the old buildings – out-of-date, mellow red bricks and variegated tiles – to the new buildings – functional, ugly, concrete block walls and asbestos roofs. Before they reached the dairy they passed a yard in which were twenty bullocks. She stopped and looked at them. 'Mr. Pattison was telling someone the other day that since you became farm manager the milk production has gone steadily upwards.'

'It's certainly risen,' he said, 'but we're running a few more cows.'

'I thought he said that the yield per cow had gone up appreciably?'

'It has done, yes.'

'So the extra cows don't explain away everything! I'm sure I'm going to push my neck out where it's not wanted, but I just can't understand people who won't admit they're good at their job when they know they are.'

'The English habit of understatement. What about you – are you good at your job?'

She was surprised by the question and apparently even disconcerted by it. She turned and studied the bullocks more intently and when one came hesitantly up to the metal gate she reached out and patted its nose. 'I get by,' she said finally.

They walked on and entered the dairy. He crossed to the huge stainless steel bulk tank, lifted up one of the lids and propped it open. He collected a milk scoop from the wall, leaned over the side of the tank, and dunked the scoop deep down several times in the milk.

'Why are you doing that?' she asked.

'The cream rises to the top. If I didn't mix it up well, you'd get too much cream.'

'I couldn't have too much, even if it is bad for my figure.'

He smiled. 'But from my point of view, you certainly could. If the butterfat content of the milk drops, the milk quality goes down a class and the milk fetches less a gallon.'

'Stark tragedy! .. You should smile more often.'

'Why?' He stood up straight, holding the scoop inside the refrigerated tank.

'Because it makes you look less completely self-reliant. It's not good for other people's egos to meet anyone completely self-reliant.'

44

He filled the gallon can. 'I'll wash this scoop, then carry the can down the road for you.'

'Were you going back down the road anyway?'

'No, but . . .'

'Then I'll take it. I'm not having you think I'm totally useless.' She took the can from him. 'Thank you and I do hope your milk quality doesn't drop.' She turned and left the dairy.

He lowered the lid of the bulk tank, checked the temperature of the milk from the outside thermometer, then leaned against the tank and looked through one of the windows to watch her walk down the farm drive. She was maturely pleasant, he decided, and the hint of challenge was intriguing.

He checked on the time. The milk lorry was late. Had the Friesian with perfect saddleback markings calved yet? How was the hedging going over on the far side of the farm?

  .   .   .   .   .

The drizzle began at three in the afternoon and turned into a cold rain at four, but by seven it had stopped and a rising westerly wind had blown away some of the clouds.

Miles went up to the Kow Kennels – made of wood and corrugated iron – and wandered along the central aisles with torch switched on as he checked on the cows. Heads turned round and bovine eyes glinted in the torchlight. Satisfied all was well, he made a shorter inspection of the three groups of bullocks and the two groups of heifers, then he returned to the house.

Originally two houses under the one roof, the building had at some time been converted into one house. There were five bedrooms and one bathroom upstairs, two living-rooms, a dining-room, a work-room and a kitchen, downstairs. He used the kitchen, the larger of the sitting-rooms, and a bedroom. Sometimes, it was like living in a deserted barracks.

He checked the television programmes in the paper and then chose to read a paperback novel of great length, well-written and entertaining. It was quite a long time before he bothered to pour himself out a drink and light a cigarette.

The first time he heard the scream, he automatically tried to identify it in terms of animal life – a rabbit, newly caught by a stoat – but even so he was disturbed enough to stop reading. The second scream convinced him that this was no animal.

He jumped to his feet, scattering the book on the floor, raced through the kitchen, where he picked up a torch, and out of the back door. There were several stout sticks just outside and he grabbed one. With torch switched on he raced round the corner of the house, down the short path to the gate, and out on to the concrete drive.

The third scream, more violent, came from his left. As he ran on, he heard a shout : 'Shut the silly bitch up.'

A hundred and fifty yards away a car was stopped by the verge and in the beam of his torch he saw a woman who struggled with two men. The men, keeping their faces turned away from him, roughly pushed her away so that she stumbled on to the verge. Then they jumped into the car, and drove off at speed. He tried to read the registration number, but the plate was plastered with mud and he was able to make out only AK and 32, together with the last letter K.

The woman came to her feet. Her mackintosh had been wrenched open, her cardigan buttons had been ripped

46

off, and her white blouse had been torn. He recognized Anne O'Reilly.

He hurried to her and put an arm round her shoulder in a gesture of comforting strength. 'It's O.K. They've gone.' His words broke through her shock and he felt her begin to tremble as she muttered : 'Oh, God! Oh, God!'

He guided her to the gate and along the path round to the kitchen and it was only when he shut the door behind them and she looked and saw they were on their own that she seemed to recover. She ran her tongue round her lips. 'They . . . they were trying to drag me into the car.' She reached up and gripped together the two halves of her blouse.

'But thank goodness they didn't succeed,' he said, in a brisk voice, trying to reduce her sense of appalled outrage. 'Are you O.K. while I phone the police? After that, I'll get you a strong drink.'

'Yes, but please . . . Just for a bit, don't leave me on my own. I'm still one hysterical female.'

He led the way into the front room. He crossed to the far corner where the telephone was, she slumped down in the nearer arm-chair. He dialled 999 and asked the operator for the police.

'You weren't able to read any more of the registration number of the car than AK, thirty-two, K?'

'No, I wasn't.'

'Can you identify the colour and make?'

'Not really, because it all happened far too quickly. But it was a dark colour, maybe blue, and a medium sized saloon somewhere in the fifteen hundred c.c. class.'

'Does the lady need a doctor and if so can you contact her own doctor?'

'Just a moment . . .' He removed the receiver from his ear. 'Do you need a doctor?' he asked her.

47

'No,' she answered, 'I'll soon be all right.'

He spoke once more to the police officer. 'She says she's O.K. and doesn't need a doctor.'

'Good. I'll see a patrol car is with you very shortly, Mr. Miles.'

He replaced the receiver. 'They're sending a car along right away.'

'When I think of what would have happened if you hadn't heard ...'

'Don't think and have a stiff drink instead. The choice is limited, I'm afraid. It's whisky or gin?'

'I'll have a whisky, please, half and half with plain water. And if you could find a safety-pin, so I don't have to go on clutching my blouse to preserve what dignity's left to me?'

He found her a safety-pin and she secured her torn blouse. When he handed her a strong whisky, she drank quickly.

She lit a cigarette and then stared at the fire, in which a log suddenly flamed up. 'It's ... it's something one's always reading about, but imagines will only happen to the other person. I've always had a sneaking feeling that in most cases the woman must have done something to egg the men on. But all I was doing was walking along the road towards the post-box at the cross-roads. The headlights picked me out and I stepped up on to the verge, then the car slowed and stopped. I just thought someone wanted to know the way. When they both got out, I was still such a fool I didn't realize the danger until one of them grabbed me. If ... if it had happened a hundred yards along the road, you might never have heard.'

'But I did hear.'

'I know, but it's not easy to forget how easy . . .' She shivered.

She was probably right, he thought, with angry hatred for the unknown men. Much further along the road and he'd have heard nothing. By now, most likely she'd have been raped, perhaps even murdered.

They heard a car stop outside and then the slam of a door. 'That's the police,' he said. 'I'll go and let them in.'

There was a knock on the seldom used front door and he went out into the tiny hall and opened this.

'Mr. Miles?' asked the young constable, his peak cap tilted jauntily on his head.

'Come on in.' Miles stepped to one side.

'How is the lady?' asked the constable, as he entered. He took off his cap. He had a square, pugnacious face.

'Not too bad, considering what happened.'

'That's good . . . Can we just hang on until my mate comes in from signing off on the blower?'

As he finished speaking, a second constable came down the path and into the house. Taller than the first, he had the same air of calm confidence.

Miles led the way into the front room where he introduced Anne. He offered them a drink, but they refused this, though the first constable accepted a cigarette. He brought a notebook from his pocket and asked Anne for her account of what had happened.

'There's nothing about their appearance you specifically noticed, then?' he asked.

She shook her head. 'Not a thing. It was all so sudden.'

'I'm afraid it always is and it's only once in a blue moon we're lucky enough to get a useful description. Were they wearing gloves?'

She thought back. 'Yes. One of them certainly was.'

'Then probably they set out with the express idea of finding someone. Did they speak?'

'No.'

'Yes, they did,' corrected Miles.

'Did they?' She shook her head. 'I'm sorry, I just don't remember.'

'Don't you worry, Mrs. O'Reilly, you're doing wonders,' said the first constable. 'Most ladies after something like this are almost incoherent.' He looked down and checked his notes, then turned to Miles and asked him to say what he'd seen and heard.

Miles told them the little he knew.

'You heard one bloke call out: "Shut the silly bitch up"? How would you describe the man's voice?'

'Coarse.' Miles rubbed his chin and stared at the fire as he thought back. 'And I think there was an accent.'

'What kind of an accent?'

'I can't give it a region, but shut was pronounced shert.'

'How was his tone of voice?'

Miles shrugged his shoulders. 'Excited is the nearest I can get.'

'Let's move on to the registration number. D'you think there's any chance of you filling in the missing letter or numbers?'

'None whatsoever. I had the beam of my torch slap on the numberplate and read all I could.'

'Ten to one, it's a nicked car anyway,' said the second constable, speaking for the first time.

'Have you had any firmer ideas on the make and model?' asked the first constable.

'I can't begin to identify either.'

'Then that takes us about as far as we're going to go.' He returned his notebook to his coat pocket. 'We'll get on the blower and give H.Q. the facts, but I'd be a liar to say there's much chance of grabbing these two blokes.' He stood up. 'If you should either of you think of anything fresh, get in touch with county H.Q., or your local divisional C.I.D. in Ardscastle.'

Miles accompanied them to the front door, said good night, then returned to the sitting-room. 'I think I'll go back now,' she said.

'Right.'

She stood up. 'You know . . .' She stopped and although he looked enquiringly at her, she did not finish what she'd been going to say.

When they reached the road, she tucked her arm round his in a gesture which plainly said she needed the comfort of physical contact. 'It's going to be a long, long time,' she said quietly, 'before I come along here without remembering.'

They said little on their walk down the road and up the left-hand fork of the drive to the house, but when there was a sudden, scrambling noise from one of the rhododendron bushes over by the fish ponds, he felt her tighten her grip on his arm.

They went round to the rear entrance and she reached up above the door and brought down a key to open the spring lock. 'I have to remember to set the alarms if I'm last in – this place is like a fortress at night. Good night and . . . and I think you must know how grateful I am.' She went in, switched on an inside light, and clicked the door shut.

6

Miles was eating breakfast when the telephone rang. Simon wanted to see him in the office at ten o'clock.

He returned to his last slice of toast and wondered why he disliked Simon quite so much as he did? It wasn't entirely Simon's faked ex-senior-officer style. No, decided Miles, it was as much the certainty that when it came to the crunch, Simon had no moral backbone whatsoever, a fact borne out by his acceptance of Miles as farm manager even though he was and always had been so clearly dead against the appointment.

Breakfast finished, he walked over to the thiry-acre field to make certain the main paddock divisions were being erercted as he'd ordered, then he returned along the road to the priory.

One of the two gardeners was digging the curving flower bed to the left of the drive and Miles noticed how very friable was the soil, which meant tons and tons of dung – which should have gone on the fields – must have been used. He remembered one of his father's favourite sayings : 'God made muck and man made artificials and man hasn't produced anything yet what don't go bloody wrong sooner or later.' His father had been quite a pessimist.

He went into the house through the back door. The cook was sitting at the large table, avidly reading a woman's magazine. ' 'Morning, Mr. Miles,' she said. She always gave him his title and in return demanded to be called Mrs. Barlowe, although she never once mentioned her husband. She put the magazine down and spoke indignantly. 'Wasn't that a terrible thing about Mrs. O'Reilly?'

'Yes, it was. How is she this morning?'

'Not too bad, but I made her stay in bed the moment I heard. I don't know what the world's coming to, and that's fact.' She sighed. 'And then I've had that horrible dago worrying me again to fry him up a load of his horrible innards because he likes the muck. Frying guts in my kitchen!'

For her, civilization ended at the English Channel. If she learned about some of the dishes he'd eaten and enjoyed in his wanderings around the Mediterranean she'd probably ban him from her kitchen.

'Soup and brandy for breakfast. Can you imagine? Guts for lunch. And squid for supper. Squid! And the mess he's made in the room he works in.'

He thought he ought to make some sort of comment. 'Really?'

'Vera's not allowed in, but she got a quick look the other day — says it was a proper pig-sty. And Mr. Pattison caught her looking and gave her such a bawling out: not like him, really.' She took a packet of cigarettes from a drawer of the table. 'Have a fag, Mr. Miles.'

'I don't think there's time, thanks — I'm meeting Simon here at ten.'

She gave him a cigarette. 'He ain't here yet and even if he is, make him wait.'

He smiled.

'You don't want to take no notice of Puffing Aggie. I'd an uncle like him — ended up in jug in Australia.'

An electric bell buzzed on the call board and she looked up to see which indicator was moving. 'Talk of the devil! Shouting for his coffee. "Black," he says, in his pebble voice, "black with exactly half a spoonful of sugar." I'm telling you, when he was young he wasn't in no position to put on such airs.'

Miles had just finished the cigarette and was preparing to leave when a man, short, heavily bearded, almost bald, complexion bronzed, entered.

'Here's the dago,' said the cook. 'I wouldn't trust him an inch.'

'I work much,' said Luque. His halting English was so heavily accented that it was very difficult to understand. 'I have much 'ungry . . .' He lapsed into Spanish. 'Barbarous, fog-bound, Philistine language. All I want is some bread and butter and a tomato and I have to strangle myself to try to get it.'

'And what's all that yak about?' snapped the cook.

'He's asking for some bread and butter and a tomato,' translated Miles.

She stared at him with surprise. 'You mean to say you understand that row?'

'I learned a little Spanish when I was knocking about the Mediterranean.'

'Well, I never!' Her tone of voice was disapproving. 'Well, you can tell this bearded goat that he can have some bread and butter if he must eat between meals, but he's getting no tomatoes. I'm not wasting them on him at the price they are now.'

Miles said in Spanish : 'There's bread and butter, but no tomatoes, Señor.'

Luque stared at Miles. 'You speak Spanish, Señor?'

'Only a little.'

He burst into a flood of words, with the breathless fervour of a man deprived of civilized speech for weeks.

'Now what's he on about?' demanded Mrs. Barlowe.

'I didn't understand it all,' replied Miles, 'but I think he's asking you to cook him a special dish which reminds him of home. It's called Frito Mallorquin. It's some sort of mixture of liver, kidney, heart, lungs, garlic . . .'

54

'Is he on about his dirty insides again? You tell him from me, he's not having that sort of muck here. I cook respectable grub.'

Miles tried to explain that Mrs. Barlowe was unfortunately too busy to do as Luque requested.

Luque looked at her with open dislike, gestured with his hands, stroked his beard, and said: 'She is the stupidest, most cross-eyed, ugly, perverse old bitch I've ever been unfortunate enough to meet.' He turned on his heels and stalked across to the doorway. 'And she can take her bread and butter and . . .' His words became lost as he stamped up the corridor.

'What did he say?' she demanded, more angry than before.

'He said he's sorry,' replied Miles.

'Well, it sounded different to that!'

Miles thanked her for the coffee and cigarette, left. He walked along the passage, past the butler's pantry, and was almost up to the office when Pattison limped into the hall. ' 'Morning, Mr. Pattison,' he said cheerfully. It was the first time he'd spoken to Pattison since starting work at the farm.

'Good morning, good morning.' Pattison was wearing a grey suit that fitted him with the exactness of expert tailoring. 'And how's everything? Is the farm doing well?'

'We're slowly licking it into shape.'

'It's nice to see all the changes: very nice. Especially the cows which are looking so shiny now. Well, I must be going. Hope everything keeps improving.' He limped across to the front door and the porch.

Miles knocked on the door of the office and went in. 'Good morning.' Simon, who was writing, made a point of not looking up and gave no acknowledgement of

Miles's presence until he said abruptly : 'You're late.'

'I've been talking to Mr. Pattison.'

Simon stood up and crossed to the fireplace where he pressed the bell push. 'Where the devil is everyone? I still haven't been brought my coffee.'

You'll be lucky, thought Miles. He sat down. 'Did you hear about Mrs. O'Reilly?'

'Vera told me.' Simon returned to his chair.

'The cook says she's not too bad today.'

'Well, it wasn't anything much.'

'That surely depends from whose viewpoint?'

Simon looked angry. 'Maybe, but we're not here to discuss that.' He opened a folder and pulled out some papers. 'Mr. Pattison is very worried.'

'About what?'

'The cost of foodstuffs. He says that consumption must be cut.'

'The cost of all compounds has gone up again in the past fortnight. In any case, we're producing more milk.'

'You were brought in to make the farm more profitable.'

'And the only way of doing that in the short term is to produce more milk.'

'A useless way if the milk you produce is uneconomic. Mr. Pattison says things have to change.'

'When I saw Mr. Pattison just now, he remarked how well everything was going on the farm.'

'He's complained to me,' snapped Simon, 'and I'm going to do something about it.'

Was Simon lying? wondered Miles. Was all this nothing to do with Pattison, but Simon was using his name?

'You're going to have to cut down on expenses,' said Simon.

'If I'm to turn this place into anything like a proper

56

farm, that's impossible. Expenses will even increase for a time because of the condition everything's been allowed to get into. Haven't you even walked around to see the extent of the neglect?'

'I check the estate regularly,' snapped Simon. 'And I know it's not nearly as bad as you're trying to make out by way of excuse . . .'

'Will you come round with me now so that I can show you?'

'I haven't the time to do something so unnecessary,' muttered Simon weakly.

'It might enable you to explain matters to Mr. Pattison.'

Simon's face reddened. He picked up the papers he'd so recently taken from the file and rammed them back in. 'That's all.'

Miles stood up and left without another word. He walked through the kitchen, empty of anyone, and out on to the drive and past the carefully clipped yew hedge. What in the hell was the total number of hours overtime he'd worked since he'd arrived? How many hours had he wrestled with the multitude of problems, trying to find solutions that weren't too costly? And who could reasonably miss the signs of growing success. Increased yield per cow, sleeker animals, improved paddocks, repaired fencing . . .

'Hullo, there! Slow down or I'll never catch you up.'

He stopped and turned to see Anne hurrying across the central lawn. She was wearing a shooting jacket over a tweed skirt and the slight wind ruffled her curly black hair.

'How are you now?' he asked.

She came to a stop. 'Patient has recovered fully and didn't even have a single nightmare.'

'Thank goodness for that. You're certainly looking better.'

'But I can't return the compliment. You were striding along looking like the wrath of God. What on earth's happened?'

Normally, he was a man who considered it a weakness to discuss his troubles with others, but his mood of resentment was so strong that he told her what had happened.

'How could he say you weren't doing wonderful things? I don't know anything about farming, but even I can see what's going on.' She started to walk and he kept pace with her. 'But I wonder if you're right to decide that it was really all Simon? I don't think he's got enough imaginative intelligence to play it as you suggest.'

'But only five minutes before, Pattison was saying . . .'

She interrupted him. 'You're forgetting, he's one of those people who suffers the desire to be loved, so he'll only be nasty through another person. I've seen that from working with him.' She looked sideways at him. 'Maybe you still don't understand, because you're so directly honest yourself?'

He shook his head, but not in denial of anything specific. He'd never bothered to ask himself whether he disliked Pattison – after all, he'd sought and accepted a favour from him – but with the essential fraudulency of the man's character revealed, he could now be certain that he did.

They reached the road and walked along this to the entrance of the concrete farm drive. One of the tractor drivers walked past with a quick look but no form of greeting. Their resentment, Miles thought, wasn't growing any less. On top of everything else, Pattison was lousy at public relations: the way he'd acted over Bert Ford had made certain the men resented their new farm manager.

'I've a confession to make,' said Anne. 'The other day I peeked into that holy of holies, the milking parlour, and I just couldn't make out what did which and to whom. I suppose you haven't time to explain things to me so I can be a bit more intelligent about it all?'

'I haven't, but I'll make it. After all, I'd better start living up to my reputation of slack inefficiency.'

'I'm . . . I'm rather sorry I told you what I did, Harry. I think you're the kind of man to remember too well.'

'Maybe.' He shrugged his shoulders.

'Are you going to get annoyed if I say there's sometimes something about the expression on your face which suggests some of your memories aren't too happy?'

'Most people have unhappy memories tucked away.'

'And are yours so unhappy?'

He hesitated, then said in a curt voice: 'My wife was killed in a car crash, together with a bloke she'd previously promised never to see again.'

'I'm very sorry. I didn't realize . . . I was once married to a man who preferred blondes, so I suppose you and I are the opposite ends of the eternal triangle. Or doesn't a triangle have ends?'

'It's a long time since I last did geometry. All I remember is that they have bloody painful points.' He resumed walking.

* * * * * *

Fertilizer prices were always rising and because of this, and because there was a discount for early purchase to prevent storage difficulties at the factories, it paid to buy before the season.

The lorry carrying hundredweight bags of compound

59

fertilizer arrived at the farm at lunch time on Friday Miles, who'd been about to open the tin which had been heating in boiling water, switched off the electric ring and left the house.

The driver of the lorry was a small, dark-eyed man with a nervous way of never keeping his gaze fixed on any one thing for many seconds. He and Miles unloaded the plastic bags, to a constant stream of complaints from him because there were not more people to help : the complaints only stopped when the last of the hundred bags was carefully stacked at the far end of the first shed in the old building. He leaned against one of the wooden pillars and watched Miles pull a tarpaulin over the bags in case the tiled roof had developed any leaks.

'You've a big place here, mate,' he said.

'It's a fair size,' agreed Miles.

'You must use a mountain of fertilizer – didn't the boss say there was another, bigger load due out before long ?'

'There's more to come, yes.'

The driver produced a two ounce tin of cigarette tobacco and from it brought out a packet of cigarette papers. He rolled a cigarette with skilful speed. 'Someone was saying your boss is worth a bomb ?'

'He's certainly not starving.

'He's loaded enough so as he wouldn't quickly miss a quid or two?'

Miles suddenly realized this was not just an aimless conversation.

The driver drew on the cigarette, then said : 'Does he take much of an interest in the farm ?'

'When he's the time.'

'You mean he's like all the other bleeding rich gentlemen farmers?' He spat. 'I know 'em. You can work your guts out, but they won't give you a thank you. If you works twenty-four hours a day, all they're interested in is why ain't you working twenty-five.'

'One can always quit.'

'Sure. Only sometime it pays to be around. Specially when the boss ain't interested in anything but making you work yourself into an early grave. Know what I mean?' For a brief second, he stared straight at Miles.

'Not really.'

'I knew the last bloke what was here. Bert and me, we had a . . . a little agreement.'

Miles was not surprised.

'Like Bert said, the boss weren't interested in what went on. And seeing as he don't pay well . . . I've got a phone – three nine three eight – give us a ring and I'll arrange things. You sign for more than what arrives and there's a quid or two for each of us.'

'Thanks,' replied Miles, 'but I don't work that way.'

'There's no risk.' He lowered his voice. 'When blokes are rich, they don't come into a shed and count the bags.'

'It's still not for me.'

'Suit yourself, mate. Work twenty-five hours a day for chicken-feed.' The driver left.

Miles heard the heavy thump of the diesel firing, then the whine of gears as the lorry backed down the roadway. Fiddling the stores delivered was a traditional way of making crooked money and one very hard to stop without checking everything. Pattison would never check anything, Simon would consider the work beneath him. It would be easy money, if one didn't mind stealing.

He left the building and returned to his house, put the water with the can back on to boil, and vaguely wondered how much Bert had made on the side.

    •   •   •   •   •

Armstrong made no secret of his dislike for hedging and ditching especially when forced to get into the ditch and chop through thick tree roots, splattering himself with sodden yellow clay. Miles ignored the continual stream of complaints, indeed hardly heard them, as he sat on the tractor and worked the ditcher, a monotonous job yet one which he liked. It was an immediately constructive job. With better drainage, the yield of grass would rise and therefore more animals would be able to graze a given area....

'It's close to knocking-off time,' said Armstrong and he dropped the blade of the slasher on to the ground and leaned on the haft.

Miles looked briefly at his watch. 'It's close, but not there yet by ten minutes.'

'It's getting too dark to see,' muttered Armstrong sullenly.

'D'you want the headlights on?'

Armstrong reversed the slasher and half-heartedly attacked a thick clump of brambles. Then he stopped again. 'There's a skirt coming across . . . It's that bit from the house.' Automatically, he smoothed down his sleek black hair. 'Got a pair of tits to tickle one's tonsils.'

Recognizing Anne at the same time as Armstrong, Miles suffered a quick anger at such unnecessary crudeness.

Anne, her cheeks reddened by the sharp wind, was wearing a thick tweed skirt, a Fair Isle sweater, a blue duffle coat which was not done up the front, and shocking yellow wellingtons. She spoke to Miles. 'I'm sorry to interrupt the good work, but the police are here and they want a quick word with you.'

'O.K. I'll come back with you . . . Sid, bring the tractor back, will you?'

'Why not leave it here for tomorrow?'

'Because I want it under cover for the night.'

Armstrong scowled his resentment.

Miles slipped off the tractor seat, which faced backwards towards the ditching unit, and climbed down to the ground. 'Where are the police now?'

'Waiting near your place,' she answered.

They walked across the field which was still sodden from the last heavy rain and their wellingtons grew clay balls which were constantly being broken off only to re-form. 'What they're checking up on,' she said, 'is if either of us has been able to remember anything fresh. I told them no, but naturally they want a direct answer from you.'

They reached a gateway and half-way through the deep mud, churned up by the repeated passages of the tractor, one of her wellingtons became stuck. She grabbed hold of him and he helped her to tug herself free. 'It's lucky you were with me,' she said, laughing, 'or I'd never have got out with dry feet. Jim used to say I could get stuck on dry concrete.'

'Jim?'

'My husband. There was a short time when we actually got on well together although now it's becoming more and more difficult to remember that.' She spoke almost wistfully. 'My brother wasn't often right, but he was about Jim.'

'What did your brother say?'

'That I'd make a bad mistake if I married Jim. We had a hell of a row over that.'

'Where does your brother live now?'

'I never really know. London, probably. He's the wild half of the family. He should have taken his own advice . . .' She nibbled her upper lip for a second. 'To hell with the past — let's talk about the future. Harry, do you like the cinema?'

63

'If there's a good film on, yes.' He unlatched the road gate and swung it open.

She passed through. 'There's a film on in Ardscastle that I've been wanting to see for a long time.'

'Consider yourself invited,' he said.

* * * * *

They went to the take-away Chinese food shop after the film show and chose half a dozen dishes which were packed in small cardboard cartons and in which the food kept warm during the six mile drive back.

They ate in the kitchen of Miles's home and drank a bottle of Spanish wine. They laughed a lot, and then, when he mentioned something which had happened to him in San Remo, she questioned him about the Mediterranean.

'I managed to get to the Costa del Sol just once – my parents weren't well off : Jim drank – and I lay on the sand amongst an army of people, shut my eyes to the concrete jungle, and imagined pine trees, vineyards, and orange groves, stretching right down to the sands and myself all alone ... I'm afraid I'm stupid : I day-dream like mad.'

'Is that being stupid? If so, I'm also witless.'

She stubbed out her cigarette. 'I guessed you were like that : I can always tell a person by the shape of his head.' She studied him intently. 'You're about to have your character analysed. You're a little too serious, but there can be times when you remember to forget your dignity. You're very conscientious. When you decide to be, you're as stubborn as a mule. And you're a dreamer. ... How's that?'

'Lousy. I'm just a failed farmer and according to my present employer, a failed farm manager.'

She spoke slowly. 'That really rankles with you, doesn't it?'

'Of course.'

She reached across the table and put her fingers lightly on his hand.

'Forget it. Pattison would criticize the Archangel Michael.' She brought back her hand. 'I hate to break up a wonderful party, but I think I ought to get back. Shall we wash up quickly?'

'I never wash up at night.'

'And nor do I. We've a lot in common, haven't we? We've both had rocky marriages, we're both lonely . . . I hope you didn't think I was impossibly forward when I suggested the flicks tonight?' Her deep blue eyes searched his face.

'If you were, I'm all for it. Even to the extent of suggesting another visit.' His voice was light.

7

In the first half of March, gales swept the southern half of the country and rain was heavy enough to cause severe flooding locally. Then, within only two days, the weather became quite balmy. Early daffodils and narcissi lifted up their storm-battered heads and showed yellow : primroses carpeted woods : catkins began to break.

At Breakthorn Priory Home Farm, the different natures of the two types of soils were more than usually apparent. The eastern land was workable, despite all the rain, the western land remained so sodden that even the ditching could not be resumed.

On the second fine day, Miles was called to the priory by Simon. Expenses, said Simon in his most avuncular manner, had not gone down since their last meeting; indeed, they'd even increased. What possible excuse could there be? Miles let his anger flow. Naturally, expenses had risen. It was the beginning of the season when most of the year's requirements had to be bought: improvements had to be paid for, as well as sweated at: if the farm hadn't been so appallingly mistreated in the past, especially by those meant to be in charge of it, not nearly so much money would now be needed to right the neglect.

'You're being insolent,' said Simon, his face twisted with rage.

'Not intentionally. I'm just not wearing the results of your incompetence.'

They discovered they disliked each other even more than they had thought.

●   ●   ●   ●   ●

Miles had arranged to meet Anne at six that evening and it quickly became clear that she was as miserable as he had been earlier angry. He said nothing until they sat down to supper in the kitchen of his house, then he asked her quietly: 'What's gone wrong, Anne?'

'I'm sorry I'm being such a wet blanket. It's nothing really.'

'Can't you tell me? I might be able to help.'

'If you could, I wouldn't let you.'

'Is it something connected with Jim?' he asked, and he was conscious of the change in his tone of voice. She'd

66

never told him what had happened to her husband after they'd parted.

'No, he's vanished. I haven't heard a word from him in over two years.'

'Then has Pattison been giving you a rough time?'

'I don't let him worry me like that . . . It's just something I'll soon get over.'

'Tell me and get it over more quickly.'

She shook her head.

'Have I said something to upset you?' he persisted.

'You? Don't be silly, Harry.'

'Then for God's sake tell me what in the hell is worrying you?'

She put her fork down and stared at the table, then spoke hesitantly. 'It's Teddy, my brother. We . . . we've always been a lot closer in spirit than most brothers and sisters. That's why it upsets me so much that he's got himself into a mess.'

'What kind of a mess is he in?'

'The usual kind of trouble for him, only this time it's a bit worse. Teddy's wild — a kind of happy wildness — and he's never settled down to doing a proper job. He's been going around for some time with a pretty rotten bunch and acting like . . . like a complete fool. I tried to tell him this was bound to mean trouble, but he wouldn't listen.'

'And there's been trouble?'

She nodded. 'He started gambling wildly. It's the old story. He made a bit and thought he was clever and then he lost everything, and more, to some pretty vicious characters. He tried to get them to wait for their money, but they've refused and if he doesn't pay them . . .' She shivered.

'Can't he borrow enough?'

'He can't borrow on his own account because he's too well known and I sent him everything I'd saved up over the past two years, but it still isn't enough.'

'I've put a little away since I've been here. Over a hundred. You can have that.'

'Oh, Harry.' She reached across the table and briefly touched him. 'No one's ever been so wonderfully kind. . . . But not even that's enough. It's . . . it's four hundred pounds I've got to find. I even went to Mr. Pattison this morning when he got back from his prison visiting and asked him for my salary in advance. I thought after doing good works, he'd be in a generous mood. Like hell! All I got was a lecture.'

He could imagine. The voice would be soft, the reasons put with hypocritical morality, the cold-blooded sympathy repelling.

'I know it's Teddy's own fault. But when you've been so close . . .' He voice broke.

He looked across, but she lowered her head so that he could no longer see her eyes. He spoke quite slowly, but very definitely. 'Anne, I'll get the money for you.'

'But how? You said you'd only a little . . .'

His voice hardened. 'Let's skip the explanations.'

'I can't let you,' she whispered. 'It's not your trouble.'

'I'm making it my trouble,' he answered.

* * * * *

It was eleven-thirty. Miles looked at his watch and then said: 'Shall I walk you home?'

She was sitting on the settee. She wore a frock that made her look younger than usual and added an extra measure of innocent freshness. 'Harry – do you really want to go back with me?'

'You surely don't think I'm going to let you go back on your own?'

'That's ... that's not what I meant.'

'I don't understand . . .' he began. Then she looked up and he saw the invitation on her face.

'Come here, Harry,' she whispered.

He moved to the settee.

'For God's sake, aren't you going to kiss me?'

Armitage had said she warmed a bloke up just to look at her. . . . She more than just warmed now: she lit fires that raged.

She turned to press herself against him. Then she kissed him with an immediate passion: their tongues met and danced together. She held his hand against her breast.

Both his hands caressed her body and she murmured words of love. Then, just before any last restraint was about to vanish, he forced himself to pull apart.

'I . . .' He stared at her frock which he'd undone to her waist.

'Harry – what's wrong?'

He spoke thickly. 'I had a very old-fashioned father who talked a lot of God. My father divided women into two kinds: the ones you bedded whenever you got the chance and the ones you married. It's something I seem to have inherited from him. Anne, I want to . . .'

'No,' she cried.

The force of her voice shocked him. 'I'm asking you to marry me.'

'Forget it. Just forget it.'

'Why?'

'Never mind why: forget it.' She buttoned up her dress clumsily so that she put the wrong button through a button-hole. She stood up. 'I'm going back.'

'Can't you tell me what's the matter?' he demanded.

She walked through to the kitchen and had taken down her mackintosh from the back of the door and put it on before he was near enough to try to help.

Usually, on the short walk back she tucked her arm around his, but she carefully walked apart from him. Nor did she speak at all until they had gone up the curving drive to the back door. She unlocked the door.

'I love you, Anne,' he said quietly.

She surprised him yet again. She put her arms round his neck and kissed him with a violence that was something other than passion. 'Forget everything,' she whispered, then she hurried inside and shut the door.

He began to walk back. She'd never mentioned a divorce, so was she still married to Jim? But a divorce was surely easy enough to obtain these days so why should the mention of marriage so upset her? Why had she been eager to go to bed with him, yet was shocked by a proposal of love? What had the final kiss signified?

.   .   .   .   .

Miles had always lived by rigid standards of honesty — another legacy from his father — yet he was determined to give Anne the money she so desperately needed even though to do so he must betray those standards. He dialled the Ardscastle number, but it was engaged. As he waited, sitting on a battered rush-bottomed chair, he wondered whether he would have found it far more difficult to swindle Pattison if Pattison hadn't proved himself so two-faced and so indifferent to another's distress? He sighed. Was he really trying to dredge up some degree of justification, no matter how warped . . . ?

He tried the number again and this time the connexion was made. 'It's Miles here, Breakthorn Priory Home Farm.' He visualized the lorry driver and his shifty eyes. 'Your firm's delivering some more compound fertilizer very soon. Any idea how much?'

There was a long pause. 'Couldn't say.'

'I believe it's ten tons.' The true figure was eighteen tons.

Another pause. 'Things changed sudden, then?'

'Very suddenly.'

'All right.' The line went dead.

Miles replaced the receiver.

8

The fertilizer arrived in the middle of lunch time on the Thursday. The driver, thought Miles, knew his job. Deliver when all the other farmhands were at lunch and not around to count the bags.

The driver, eyes more restless than ever, watched his approach, then visually checked the drive and the road.

'I'm playing it straight,' said Miles, appreciating the harsh irony of his words.

The driver fidgeted with his pointed right ear. He remained uneasy. 'You changed so sudden, mister.'

'As I told you over the phone, circumstances changed suddenly. I need some money quickly.'

'I've ten ton on the lorry.' He took two green delivery

tickets from his breast pocket and handed them across, then watched Miles's face and his eyes suddenly held steady.

One delivery ticket was made out for eighteen tons of compound fertilizer, the other for ten. Miles crumpled up the second ticket and put it in his coat pocket, signed the first one. 'Where's the cash?'

The driver held out his hand for the ticket.

'Let's make it a swop.'

The driver left and crossed to the cab of the lorry and hauled himself up inside. When he returned, he took from his breast pocket a grubby brown envelope. 'There's two hundred and eighty inside, mister.'

Miles handed over the delivery ticket and pocketed the envelope without checking the contents. 'O.K. Let's unload.'

•   •   •   •   •

After he'd finished work that evening, Miles walked along to the priory. Against a darkening sky, the old priory with its tall walls of ragstone looked sombre, almost menacing in character, and it was easy to imagine that it had once enclosed a community of monks in whom piety had slowly grown into fanaticism.

He went into the house and through to the kitchen where he found Vera. 'Hullo, Harry.' Unlike Mrs. Barlowe, she always used Christian names. 'It's warmer, ain't it, which is a good thing. . . . Come to see Anne, have you?'

'If she's free?'

'She'll be free, all right, hearing as you're looking for her.' Vera, as if to compensate for her own celibate life ('Who'd want to court me, looking like I do?') saw romance everywhere. 'You sit down and I'll go up and tell her you're here. And if you feel like a sip, there's a bottle tucked away behind the washing machine.'

He was surprised to discover, while he waited, that he was nervous. Good God, he thought, didn't age ever cool a man down? He heard footsteps, but only one person's. Vera returned into the kitchen and the expression on her ugly face was one of perplexity. 'She says she's got a headache, Harry, so she can't come down.'

He spoke initially without really meaning to. 'A sudden diplomatic headache? . . . Do me a favour, Vera. Go back up and tell her I've something for her brother and all she need do is come down and collect it.'

'All right. I can't think why . . .' She left.

When he next heard footsteps, there were two sets. Vera who led the way in was smiling broadly, Anne who followed was looking almost sullen.

'I've some work to do in me room,' said Vera, happily unaware that no excuse had ever been more transparently a lie. She winked at Miles before turning and leaving, firmly shutting the door into the passage after herself.

Anne sat down in one of the wooden chairs. 'What do you want?' she asked bleakly.

'Surely Vera told you that I've brought something for your brother?'

She said nothing.

He was chilled by her blank indifference. He took an envelope from his pocket and handed it to her. She dropped it into her lap.

'Aren't you going to look inside?'

With an obvious reluctance, she looked inside the envelope.

'There's the money he needs. Send it him right away and you can stop worrying.'

She still said nothing. When he next spoke, his voice was sharp. 'Anne — there's enough there to get Teddy out of trouble. Isn't that what you were so desperate for?'

She looked at him, her blue eyes filled with an expression he couldn't read and she shook her head. 'I told you to forget everything.' Her voice was so low it was almost a whisper. 'Why couldn't you?'

'Because you were so terribly distressed.'

'But . . .' She stopped.

'Look, things can't be quite as bad as all that. It's a nice night, so put on your coat and come for a walk and talk things over. Talking can help sometimes.'

She shook her head. 'I . . . I've got a bad headache.' She tried to sound more convincing. 'I'm feeling rotten enough to go to bed.'

'When will I see you next?' he asked, determined to break down her reserve.

She shook her head. 'I don't know. But . . .' She looked down at the envelope and her voice softened. 'Harry — I'll never forget what you've done for me.' She turned and left, running in her haste to be gone.

He walked through the kitchen and out. He'd thought the money would be a wonderful surprise for her, but instead it seemed merely to have distressed her even more than she had been.

•   •   •   •   •

Miles had expected some word from Anne over the week-end, but there was none. On Monday afternoon he met Vera as he was returning along the road from Valley Field. Vera was dressed in her best clothes and, as she immediately told him, on her way to visit her great friend, Beth, who lived down in the village.

'How is Anne?' he asked, as casually as he could while conscious that Vera would not accept it as a casual question.

'But didn't she tell you?' Vera showed her astonishment. 'She's gone away for a couple of days. She told me she'd a bit of trouble in the family, so I suppose she's gone to see what she can do.'

She might, he thought resentfully, have taken a few minutes off to tell him what she was doing.

'It ain't long, Harry. Mr. Pattison said she was coming back Wednesday night. Bit cross, he was.' She chuckled 'He don't like having his routine upset, and that's fact . . . Now don't you go on worrying. Everything'll be all right in the end.' Vera never read a book, went to a film, or watched a television play, unless reasonably certain the ending was going to be happy. 'By the way, did you read the news this morning?'

'What news?'

'About that Spanish bloke, Miguel, what was here and so upset cook with all the horrid things he wanted to eat. He's dead. Gone and got himself blown up in Madrid.'

'Blown up?'

'Seems like it was them Baskets what the Spanish are always having trouble with and he was in the way when a bomb went up. Awful, ain't it? No one's safe these days. Gave me quite a turn, I can tell you. Wasn't more'n a couple of weeks when he was in the house and making such a terrible mess. Took me hours and hours to clean up the room afterwards. . . . Never know what's going to happen, do you?'

'That's true.'

'Well, I must be getting on. Beth's having this tea party and I'm cutting the sandwiches.'

He said good-bye and walked on and his sense of

75

resentment grew. Why couldn't Anne have at least let him know she was going away for a couple of days, to give her brother the money? Even a note would have been better than nothing ...

9

Wednesday morning suggested a day of mixed weather. There was a sharp breeze with a touch of cold to it to remind people winter might not be finally over and done with, black clouds to the east, but blue skies to the west. Miles guessed the day would be predominantly dry, if not sunny, and he sent two tractors out to plough the twenty-acre field, now surprisingly dried out, and order-ed the other two men (the cowman, Andy, did not work in the fields) to make final preparations for turning the cows out into the first of the paddocks.

He went through to the office – a room in the old buildings – and checked on the breeding chart on the near wall. Two cows he'd seen bulling out in the yard were, the chart confirmed, bulling for the third time. Had Andy noticed them and already got them down for the A.I.?

Miles saw a man walk past the office window and re-cognized Simon. He stepped out of the office, left the building, went round the corner, and called out: 'Are you looking for me?'

Simon stopped and turned. He was dressed in a cavalry twill coat, a crested blazer, striped shirt with matching tie, and black flannel trousers. 'Yes, Miles, I was looking for you.' His tone of voice was very clipped.

'Shall we go down to the house where it'll be warmer?'

'No. We'll go into the shed where the fertilizer is stored.'

Miles knew a sudden sick apprehension: there was no mistaking the note of triumph in the other's voice. 'We've got fertilizer in two places . . .'

'Whichever shed the last two loads are stored in.'

It had to be coincidence, Miles desperately told himself, not believing it could be. They walked back along the concrete drive, past the old cowshed to the end wing. He unlatched the heavy wooden door with massive cast-iron hinges and swung this open. Simon pushed past him, assuming with disdainful certainty that Miles would wait for him to pass through first.

The fertilizer now took up half the available floor space and the tarpaulin barely covered the top of the pile. Several sparrows flew up from the tarpaulin to the eaves, then flew through a gap where a brick had crumbled away.

Simon stopped in front of the fertilizer and stood facing it, legs akimbo. 'How many tons are there?'

'I'm not certain.'

Simon's expression became contemptuous. He brought from his pocket two white-copy delivery notes and fanned them out in his right hand. 'Is any left over from last year?'

'No. What was left has already gone out on the ground.'

'So there are two loads here – one of five tons and one of eighteen?'

Miles jammed his hands in his pockets. The lorry driver must have been found out, probably when he tried to sell the stolen eight tons. The bloody fool he thought with bitter anger.

77

'Are there twenty-three tons of compound fertilizer here?'

He could try to bluff it out, but that would only prolong Simon's pleasure because Simon would order him to count the bags. . . . 'No, there aren't.'

'I see. What exactly is there?'

'Fifteen tons.'

'Your signature is on the delivery notes for twenty-three tons. Where are the missing eight tons?'

Miles didn't answer.

'In other words, the old, old swindle.' Simon spoke with scornful satisfaction.

Miles shrugged his shoulders.

'What else have you stolen since you've been here?'

'Nothing.'

'Really? Perhaps Mr. Pattison should think himself lucky that having granted you a great favour – against my advice – you content yourself with only stealing a mere eight tons.'

'You can skip the cheap sarcasm.'

'It'll pay you to keep a civil tongue in your head.'

Would Anne have the sense to keep quiet about the reason for the swindle? wondered Miles bleakly. There'd be nothing gained by dragging anyone else into the mess.

'You're lucky,' said Simon spitefully. 'Mr. Pattison still feels himself under some sort of an obligation to you – despite what has happened. He therefore is not reporting your conduct to the police, which I think . . .'

'What you think couldn't be more obvious.'

'With perfect justification. You have a week's notice, starting immediately. You'll be granted no references. Finally, don't get any fresh ideas – I'll be keeping a very close watch on everything.'

'That'll be something new.' Miles took a pack of

cigarettes from his pocket and lit one, breaking his own rule about no smoking in the sheds. He noticed his hands were shaking.

Simon, discovering that he couldn't find anything more to say, turned and stamped out of the shed. Miles followed him out, but turned in the opposite direction to go round the old buildings, past the huge open slurry pit, to the new buildings. The cows, some lying or standing in their Kow Kennels and peacefully chewing the cud, others feeding at the face of the self-feed silage, gave much better milk averages than when he'd first come. The heifers and bullocks were showing a better growth rate. The two Dutch barns, now almost empty, would be filled to overflowing this summer because of the improvement to the grass. The hedges were gradually being cut back, the ditches cleaned out. . . . His skill, dedication, imagination, had begun to work a near miracle of rebirth. Caught up in the challenge, he had virtually forgotten that originally he'd only come here to make enough money to hurry back to the sun. . . . And he'd destroyed everything for the sake of a woman's happiness.

He kicked a lump of dried clay, scattering it into many pieces which rattled against the side of the nearest wall. He didn't regret having done what he'd done – just having been caught. That, he thought with cynical self-dislike, must be the cry of every crook brought to justice.

A man came round the Dutch barn, saw him, and crossed to where he stood. 'We're running out of barbed-wire, Harry. I reckon we need another four rolls.' Len was the oldest of the tractor drivers.

He jerked his mind back to the trivialities of life. 'I ordered a dozen rolls a week back, but they'd none in stock.'

'There ain't never anything in stock these days.' Len

79

shifted his weight from one foot to the other, hawked and spat, took a tobacco tin from his pocket. 'Care for the makings?'

'Thanks.' Miles rolled himself a cigarette with the clumsiness of a man who usually smoked tailor-mades.

Len spoke hurriedly. 'The missus was wondering if you'd come for a bite of supper?'

Miles lit the cigarette. 'I'd like that, Len.'

'How about Saturday or Sunday?'

'Either day'll suit me fine.'

'Saturday, then: the telly's a bit better.' Len rolled his own cigarette, lit it, and walked back the way he'd come.

Life was a joker, thought Miles. He'd at last made a friendly contact with one of the farmhands, but only after he'd been sacked.

He kicked another clod to pieces.

. . . . .

Miles was a sound sleeper who was undisturbed by any regular noise yet who awoke immediately to any unusual one, even if not loud. He awoke that night. The curtains were made of cheap material and were unlined and as he stared into the darkness beyond the foot of the bed he seemed to catch a momentary shifting of the complete blackness. He heard a shout.

He climbed out of bed, switched on the bedside light, and crossed the bare wooden floor. He drew the curtains. Slightly to the right, beyond tall trees that were momentarily outlined, a tongue of flame reared up and then died back. Christ! he thought, Breakthorn Priory was on fire.

80

10

Flames were spearing out of windows on both main floors, but only a few rooms on the third floor – a warren of small maids' rooms – had yet caught alight. The newly arrived fire engine was parked on the left-hand arm of the drive and the firemen were rigging up a hose and trying to get it into operation with a certain lack of cohesion of effort which suggested there was as yet no fire officer present senior enough to take effective command.

Miles saw the chauffeur and ran across the lawn. 'What happened?' he demanded hoarsely.

'God knows, mate. My missus has been feeling rotten all night and I got up to get her some aspirins and looked out and there was the flames. I phoned nine nine nine and came up, but there wasn't no chance of getting near the house.'

'Who's escaped?'

The chauffeur, bewildered by events, shook his head.

It was impossible to believe anyone still in the house – with the third floor out of use – could be alive. Miles watched a jagged flame surge out of one of the second floor windows. Where had Vera and Mrs. Barlowe slept? Had everyone been overcome while still in bed? And then, with a horrible, sick shock, he remembered Vera's telling him that Anne was returning on Wednesday night. Terror made him breathless, as if his lungs were being squeezed. Frantically, he looked at his watch. Half past four. The last train from London arrived at Ardscastle at about eleven. If she'd travelled down, she'd have arrived at between eleven-twenty and eleven-thirty . . .

Headlights rounded the drive and another pump unit was followed by a fire officer's car and then a patrol car.

Before long, orders were being shouted and the firemen worked with a new-found orderliness. Four hoses were being played on to the west end of the house, trying to hold back the fire's final advance. A ladder was raised and, despite the appalling heat, placed against the end of the house. A man in fireproof clothing climbed the ladder, sprayed with ricocheting water from jets aimed to either side of him. He reached one of the very few windows on the second floor not yet shattered, smashed the glass with his axe, and leaned inside. He withdrew immediately. A long tongue of flame rolled out.

Miles saw, being tended by the side of a patrol car, a woman who lay on a stretcher and had over her a couple of blankets. He ran across. As the policeman looked up, Miles recognized Mrs. Barlowe. She was plainly suffering from shock and without her teeth in her mouth she looked like a cruel caricature of herself.

Miles's voice was hoarse. 'Mrs. Barlowe, did Anne come back last night?'

She looked straight up at him, but made no answer.

'Can't get nothing out of her,' said the constable. 'We've called for a doctor by blower.'

'Who else escaped from the house?'

The constable slowly stood up. 'I've not heard of anyone else getting out,' he said reluctantly.

Miles looked back at the house and saw the top floor was now flaming. He ran round to the south side because survivors might just have congregated there. The flames lit up the lawn, the water-lily filled pond, the tall outside walls of the old priory, and showed him there was no one there. He continued round.

The stark horror of the situation suddenly reminded him of the sinking of the *Oakmore*. He remembered the hideously burned greaser who'd plummeted into the sea.

He imagined Anne screaming, her burned flesh peeling away . . . She must have been detained in London, he thought wildly.

Armstrong walked up to where he stood. 'It's a fair old bonfire, ain't it? Just right for the fifth of November.'

Miles silently cursed his callous facetiousness, even though recognizing this was merely a way of covering up the horrified shock he felt.

'D'you hear the cook got out?' went on Armstrong, completely unaware of Miles's emotions. 'They don't reckon anyone else did. Seems like someone came back late at night – that'll be a trip they'll wish they never made'.

'How d'you know that?'

'Max was saying : heard the car drive in and out.'

Miles saw the chauffeur again and ran across to where he was now standing. 'Did you hear a car come in late last night?'

The chauffeur was plainly embarrassed, well aware that gossip amongst the staff said Miles had been seeing a lot of the secretary – and she'd been due to return from London the previous night.

'What time did the car arrive?' demanded Miles.

'About half eleven. I heard it drive in and go on up to the house. Then it came back and drove off in the direction of Ardscastle.' The chauffeur struggled to offer some form of hope. 'It came back smartly so maybe it was just a car took a wrong turning.'

Miles turned away, sickly wondering how anyone could conceivably pass the ornate entrance and go all the way up to the house before realizing he'd taken a wrong turning? The drive from Ardscastle took twenty minutes. Five minutes to get from the train to the taxi rank . . .

A small section of roof at the eastern end crashed in.

A volcano of sparks shot up into the night sky, pursued by writhing tongues of fire.

.   .   .   .   .   .

By daybreak, the fire was under control and being damped down. Five pump units were at work, pouring water through the shattered windows into the glowing mounds of rubble inside. Initially, the water was turned into steam which rose in white clouds that entwined with the black smoke, then it seemed to win its battle and extinguish the fire to leave the twisted rubble a sodden, dead mess : but when the jet of water moved on, as often as not the black smoke rose again.

Anyone ignorant of the spectator appeal of catastrophe would have been amazed that so many people should have bothered to get out of bed early to visit the dismal scene : half the village seemed to be there. Two uniform constables were having to carry out crowd control.

A uniform superintendent was in charge of the preliminary investigations. Routine enquiries into how many people had been sleeping in the house, how many had escaped, and the probable cause of the fire. He was impatiently waiting to hear how soon the doctors at Ardscastle General Hospital would allow the cook to be questioned.

The firemen were tired, wet, cold, and dispirited. They hated a fire which defeated them so completely. The men from the local village fire station, the first to arrive and all volunteers, were also sick at heart : none of them had previously fought a fire in which people had been killed.

Two reporters, from rival local newspapers, were eagerly questioning everyone and getting in the way. Both of them had private agreements with the national papers and were paid extra for anything published in those papers.

Miles, chin heavily stubbled, eyes bloodshot from smoke and fatigue, lit the last cigarette in the pack. One of the firemen had told him – without emotion – that as soon as the interior of the house had cooled down sufficiently, he and his companions would be going in to try and find the location of the corpses. Routine. But somewhere there might be Anne's body, blackened and unrecognizable . . .

He threw the cigarette to the ground and stamped it out. If only he could find out for certain. If there was no hope, then let him know this now so that he no longer tortured himself with the belief that there still remained one chance in a hundred . . .

A middle-aged woman, plump, with a pleasant, round face, came up to him. 'Come back to our place, Harry, and have a bite of something.'

He gave no indication that he had heard Len's wife.

'You can't do nothing here,' she said softly.

He could do nothing here but torture himself further, yet he knew a terrible reluctance to leave.

She took hold of his arm and led him across the grass to the right-hand sweep of the drive.

.   .   .   .   .

The uniform superintendent was a man close to retirement who had started his career as a radical and was ending it as a reactionary. Sad experience had convinced him that major crime was the obvious sign of an evil so great it needed cutting out with ruthless efficiency.

He spoke with a deep, tuneful voice : when young, he'd been a passable baritone. 'You reckon it'll be another two to three hours before you can get in among the rubble?'

'At the very minimum,' replied the station officer, a tall, thin, dyspeptic man. 'It's still as hot as hell in parts.'

The superintendent looked at his wrist watch. 'I might get back for a bath and something to eat, then ... Any comments on the fire, yet?'

The station officer looked at the smouldering ruins in which only the main walls and one roof at the west end still stood. 'It was an unusually intense fire, considering the maximum time it could have been burning when first discovered. The chauffeur said he didn't see any sign of trouble at a quarter to four, or thereabouts, yet by four-fifteen the whole place was a blazing inferno. Private houses don't usually go up that fast.'

'Arson?'

The station officer shrugged his shoulders. 'I'm not saying anything as definite as that at this stage.'

The superintendent grunted. 'But it sounds as if I'd better call out C.I.D.' He drew his hand across his forehead in a gesture of tiredness. 'From all accounts, there was a lot of valuable stuff inside. It's going to be a costly fire for someone.'

    ·   ·   ·   ·   ·

The detective constable was led by the nurse across to the curtained-off bed. The nurse introduced him and then withdrew. He sat down on the chair. 'Sorry to have to bother you, Mrs. Barlowe. How are you feeling?'

'Not so bad,' she answered, her voice slurred because of her lack of teeth. Embarrassed by this lack, she kept her head turned away from him.

'The doctor said you were very brave ... Mrs. Barlowe, can you tell me who was sleeping in the house last night?'

'There was Mr. Pattison, me, and Vera . . . What's happened to Vera?'

'I'm afraid she's not known to have escaped.'

'I liked Vera.' It was a simple statement, filled with heartbreaking sorrow.

'What time did you go to bed?'

'Vera and me was a bit late because of the telly. Mr. Pattison had his hot chocolate at ten, like always, and Vera took it to him. Then when the programme was over, we went to bed.'

'Did you go straight up?'

'I had a look round in all the downstairs rooms to make certain everything was all right, first.'

'And you locked up?'

'All except the back door, seeing Mrs. O'Reilly was coming back. And I left the outside alarms off so as she wouldn't start 'em up when she opened the door.'

'Did you hear Mrs. O'Reilly return?'

'No, but I sleep sound and anyways, she slept in a different part of the house to Vera and me.'

'I've brought a sheet of paper, Mrs. Barlowe, hoping you'll be able to draw a rough sketch of the house on it and show where you, Vera, Mrs. O'Reilly, and Mr. Pattison, all slept. D'you think you're up to doing that now?'

'I reckon.' She struggled to a sitting position.

She drew a surprisingly detailed plan of the second floor, marking the occupied bedrooms. When he asked her to sketch out the ground floor as well, she did that.

'That's great, Mrs. Barlowe.' He folded the paper and put it in the back of his notebook. 'Last of all, can you tell me what happened when you woke up?'

She'd had a bad dream: a nightmare really. She'd awakened and, as always when she awoke during the night, her first emotion had been fear: maybe Mrs.

87

O'Reilly had forgotten to set the alarm and a burglar had crept in. Then she'd heard the roar and smelled smoke. She'd climbed out of bed, crossed to the door and opened it, and been faced by a wall of flame : the heat had been unbelievable. She'd only just saved her life by slamming the door. Her room overlooked the roof of the dairy. Climbing out of the window, she'd been able to drop down to the sloping roof and from there to the ground, at the cost of a slightly twisted ankle. Despite the ankle, she'd hurried across the grass and when she'd reached the old mulberry tree and turned, she'd seen that her room was already engulfed in flames.

The D.C. finished writing. 'You've really been through it,' he said, in a sympathetic voice.

· · a · ·

The P.C., not long sworn in after having been a police cadet, was brusquely smart. 'Did any of your chaps pick up a fare last night from the last London train?'

The bald-headed, short-sighted man who sat in front of the unstained desk before the window of the office outside the station on the down side, said : 'Half a mo.' He picked up a foolscap sheet of paper and looked down it. 'One fare, off the eleven three, out to Breakthorn Priory. One quid fifty.'

'Can I have a word with the driver?'

'He's home now, seeing he's on nights. I'll give you his address, shall I?'

· · · · ·

The taxi driver was middle-aged and rather obsequious. 'Yes, I remember, Constable. A very nice woman. Gave me a pleasant tip : very pleasant, considering these days

88

people don't tip as they used to, and who can blame 'em with taxes – not taxis, eh ? – so high.'

'Can you describe her?'

'Well, I suppose, only I'm not very good at it, you'll understand, even at the best of times. And the light ain't so good outside the station and she was wearing a hat what covered a good bit of her face. Not tall, just middling. Not far off the plumpish side. And where her hat didn't hide her, she'd black curly hair.'

'Did she speak?'

'Didn't say nothing on the journey. I tried to chat, like, but when she kept quiet, I kept quiet – good relations with the customer, see. When we arrived at this enormous place, more like a castle than a house, she said something about being real quiet and not waking Mrs. . . . Mrs. . . . Mrs. Barlowe, that was the name.'

.   .   .   .   .

The world didn't stop for tragedies, no matter how appalling. The farm remained. Animals had to be milked, the decision taken as to whether to go out to grass, the isolation pens needed to be cleaned out and disinfected, Oak field must be disced down . . .

At five to one, Miles went along the road, through the ornate gateway, and up the drive. He passed round the knot of onlookers and was then stopped by a uniform constable. He identified himself and the constable let him continue.

Half a dozen men were clambering over the sodden rubble, gingerly examining what lay beneath. The firemen wore thigh length waders and the two civilians were in once white overalls and wellingtons.

Miles saw a senior policeman near the porch – looking

grotesque now as it had hardly been damaged and its exotic extravagance framed only ruins – and he crossed over. 'Can you tell me something, please?' His voice was uneven.

The superintendent, round-faced, strong-chinned, replied courteously : 'Yes, of course – if I can.'

'Have you found anyone dead yet?'

'No. It's taking much longer than we expected for everything to cool down. Are you worried about someone in particular?'

'Mrs. O'Reilly.'

'Could you say for certain whether she returned last night?'

'No. But . . . the chauffeur says a car drove in at eleven-thirty and very soon drove out again. If she caught the last train back...' He stopped.

The superintendent sadly wondered how long it would be before there was positive confirmation that she had returned in that car?

.   .   .   .   .

Detective Inspector Crane had gained his promotions at unusually early ages and fellow members of the force were inclined to say this fact had made him swollen headed. It hadn't, but equally it hadn't done anything to lessen his self-confidence. He had a thinly featured face – thin nose, thin lips, thin cheeks – but unusually large brown eyes under bushy eyebrows. One of his D.C.s had once described him as looking like a fakir who'd swallowed a bottle of hair restorer.

He listened to the report from Detective Constable Retson, a man approaching middle age who would be retiring soon. When Retson finished, he said : 'Over there, where the two blokes are standing? Is the head male or female?'

'There's really no saying at the moment and it's going to be a job to get down to the body.'

Crane looked at Mrs. Barlowe's sketch of the downstairs of the house, turned it over to compare the position where the body lay with the occupied bedrooms above. The two didn't appear to match. The sketch might be proportionately wrong or one of the victims might have escaped from a bedroom only to be caught along a corridor.

Crane watched Retson trudge back to the shattered building. He would go over soon, to see the body exactly as it had been found, but for the moment he wanted to continue to get the feel of the scene. His nature was down-to-earth, yet at the same time he was a great believer in taking time off to appreciate an atmosphere. What atmosphere was there here? He reviewed the main facts. A fire of devastating violence, described as having reached its greatest intensity unnaturally quickly. A millionaire (almost certainly) dead, together with a maid and (very probably) a secretary. An art collection which was worth a fortune, plus a whole load of antiques, burned.

He walked slowly towards the house and climbed inside. He stumbled over the uneven piles of rubble to where Retson was working with one other man. 'Straight down, sir,' said Retson.

Crane studied the burned head, closing down that part of his mind which would have liked to be horrified by the scene. It was impossible to judge the sex of this victim, but surely there was just a hint of maleness to the head?

There was a call from his left. Two firemen who'd been using crowbars to shift some rubble had obviously found something of importance. He climbed across to them.

'There's another,' said the elder of the two.

Lying on its side was a second body and because of the way in which it had been burned he could be certain this one was female. He again referred to Mrs. Barlowe's sketch of the house. They were standing below where had been the bedroom in which Mrs. O'Reilly had slept.

.   .   .   .   .

The tragedy had the effect of immediately accelerating the more friendly feeling the other farm workers had begun to show Miles. Len's wife insisted he had supper with them and Wesley wanted to know if someone was giving him a meal because otherwise there was something to eat in his place.

He had supper at Len's and was smoking a cigarette after the meal when there was a quick knock on the door and Ray Eager entered. 'Have you heard . . .' he began excitedly and then he saw Miles and stopped abruptly.

'You're just in time for a cup of tea, Ray,' said Len's wife hastily.

'No, thanks all the same. Me and Doll's just had some.'

Miles said: 'What's the latest news? I noticed they've got the spotlights on to help digging. Have they just got another body out?'

Ray nodded.

'Who?'

'They ain't certain.'

'Male or female?'

'Female.'

'Vera?'

'She couldn't've been Vera,' blurted out Ray, 'she'd got all her fingers.'

Miles remembered the missing little finger of Vera.

'They ain't certain who she is . . .' began Ray, not realizing that his attempts to cushion the truth were only adding to the pain.

Miles abruptly left the kitchen and walked into the darkness. He wished he could find relief in tears, but his eyes remained dry : the icy pain in his heart grew.

I I

Miles was watching the cows being herded out to grass for the first time that season – some of them were frisky enough to cause both Len and Ray to curse almost continuously – when a thickset man with a face like a prizefighter's came up the farm drive to him. 'Mr. Miles?'

'Yes.'

'I'm Detective Sergeant Oliveland. Would it be possible to have a quick chat?'

'All right.' Miles watched the last of the cows go through the gateway. Within forty-eight hours the milk yield would begin to increase, even though the grass wasn't as yet really nutritious. He looked up at the sky. Too much rain from now on, turning the heavy-soiled paddocks into bogs, would be disastrous ...

Oliveland said : 'I'm afraid it's about Mrs. O'Reilly.'

He flinched. Just for a very short while he had been able to forget. 'Yes?' he said dully.

'We're trying to trace and contact next-of-kin.'

Death was said to be final, but this was a terrible mistake. For those who'd known and loved a person who died, death lasted a long, long time. He spoke wearily. 'I know hardly anything about her background other than that she had a brother.'

93

'Do you have the brother's address?'

'Neither his address, not even his surname. His Christian name was Teddy.' Briefly, he added that Anne's husband's name had been Jim, but he'd no idea if there'd been a divorce.

'She didn't talk about things much?'

'She'd obviously had a rough time and didn't want to be reminded of it.'

'I know. Some people get all the kicks in life,' Oliveland said with quiet sympathy. 'Our immediate trouble is to get an identification. I'm afraid we're going to have to ask you to help.'

Miles briefly closed his eyes.

'She was burned quite badly so I don't think we'll have to ask you to view the body.' Oliveland spoke quite naturally, the only way in which such shocking facts could be dealt with. 'But there was a ring. Did Mrs. O'Reilly wear any rings?'

Miles painfully thought back. 'She had a plain gold ring on her marriage finger.'

'No engagement ring?'

'I never saw her with one.'

'Did you ever examine the gold wedding ring?'

'No.'

'You wouldn't know if there was anything engraved on it?'

'No, I wouldn't.'

'Did she go to any of the local dentists while she worked here? We sometimes make an identification by teeth.'

'For God's sake, you know it had to be her.'

'The identification has to be as complete as possible. What about dentists?'

'She never mentioned going to any.'

'What colour was her hair?'

94

'Black, with tight curls.'

'Her height?'

'I suppose it was about five foot six or seven.'

'Was she thin or fat?'

'Well built.'

The detective sergeant looked down at his notebook. 'D'you have any idea what kind of nightclothes she usually wore?'

'No, I bloody well don't.'

'I'm sorry, Mr. Miles. These are all questions we have to ask.'

'What goddamn difference does it make what she wore?'

'Part of her body was resting against some brickwork and a small square of clothing was saved from destruction.'

In his mind, he saw her cowering against a wall . . .

'Perhaps you'd come and see the ring now? It's better got over and done with, once and for all.'

They really crucified you, thought Miles despairingly.

The mortuary was in Ardscastle, at the back of the parish church. From outside, the place looked like a ramshackle social hall: inside, it had been modernized and there was a small waiting-room which even had a few out-of-date weekly magazines on a table.

Oliveland left Miles in the waiting-room, returned very soon with a small white cardboard box which he opened. Inside was a plain gold ring, tarnished by fire.

'It could be,' muttered Miles.

'Thanks.' Oliveland closed the box. He knew that on the inside of the ring were engraved the words, 'To Anne, with all my love, Jim'.

●　　　●　　　●　　　●　　　●

Crane picked up the internal phone on his desk and asked the duty sergeant to organize two coffees with plenty of sugar. He replaced the receiver. 'You'd think sugar here was still rationed.'

'The canteen people probably like to take a regular supply home.' Wesley Pace, investigating officer for the county fire brigade, was a handsome man who wore clothes which cost more than his wife said he could afford.

Crane picked up a quarto sheet of paper. 'This is a report on the position of the three bodies. Have you seen it?'

'Not yet.'

'Keep this copy, if you like.'

Pace took the paper and read through the report. 'So there was a fire extinguisher close to the body of Pattison. Have you discovered where it came from?'

'Probably from the glass cupboard on the north wall of the secondary sitting-room. The cook says the place was stiff with extinguishers.'

'But his body was in the centre of the main sitting-room so it looks like he grabbed the extinguisher and tried to put out the fire. More courage than prudence unless then it was only a tiny fire. But if only a tiny one, how come it spread so violently?'

'That's what I'm about to ask you.'

There was a knock on the door and a cadet came in with a tray on which were two coffees. 'Sergeant says that's ten pence, sir, and could he have it now.'

Crane took a tenpence piece from his pocket and handed it over. The cadet left. Crane passed one mug across, together with the sugar bowl. 'Are you ready yet to talk about arson?'

Pace stirred his coffee. 'First, what's the news on the insurance front?'

'The five major paintings were insured for just over a million, a collection of gold frogs for a hundred and twelve thousand, and sundry other antiques for another hundred thousand.'

'Is everything gone?'

'The paintings certainly have. They hung in the main sitting-room and we've found a bit of one of the frames with a couple of square inches of canvas still on it. That's been sent for testing. The gold frogs were in the strong-room and your blokes say that can't be opened yet awhile because they're not certain it's cooled down enough.'

'It's an expensive fire, then?'

'Yeah. The kind of expensive fire an owner sets when he's in trouble and likes the look of the insurance money. But Pattison was trying to douse the fire with the extinguisher and he's the bloke who'd have benefitted from any insurance swindle.'

'So maybe it isn't arson?'

'I'm still waiting for you to tell me about that,' replied Crane, a shade impatiently. He found Pace's studied casualness irritating.

'Let's have a recap on some of the evidence. All downstairs windows and doors were shut and locked – as required by the conditions of insurance. All glass so far checked was shattered by heat, not impact. The alarm system had two circuits, one to the main sitting-room and the strong-room, one to the rest of the downstairs. We've found the control panel and both circuits were alive at the time of the fire, as they should have been after Mrs. O'Reilly's return. The one to the main sitting-room had not gone off which must be because fire had already destroyed the wiring by the time Pattison opened up the main sitting-room.

'Now we have to consider the nature of the fire.' Pace paused.

Like a bloody schoolmaster, thought Crane.

'There are two possible reasons for suspicion. The fire raced through the house and reached major intensity in a suspiciously short time. More important, the firemen who were first on the scene seem to be reporting two separate centres of intensity which would mean two seats of fire.'

'Seem to be?'

'They're the volunteer crew from the local village and the excitement of a real fire went to their heads.' Pace spoke in a sardonic tone of voice. 'They contradict each other on this point.'

'Would two seats of fire make arson a certainty?'

'As near as you can get without definite proof. You know that I've sent various samples up to our laboratories for testing for paraffin? With a fire so fierce, you don't get many traces left, but I tried the old trick of rubbing bread on some wood which hadn't been completely consumed – some of the soot deposited on the walls had the appearance of a paraffin base – and I'd say there was the taste of paraffin there. So unless the cook says they used to coat exposed wood with paraffin against worm – which I've met more than once – your decision to search the rubble with a fine tooth comb is likely to prove fully justified.'

Crane drained his cup, drew on the cigarette, then stubbed it out in an already full ash-tray. 'How would you list the most common motives for arson?'

'In a private house? Insurance fraud, revenge, pyromania, in that order.'

Crane thought it unlikely some business associate would have come down and set the fire – if this was arson, the arsonist had obviously known a great deal about the house's routine and alarm system. A disgruntled employee – one of the farm workers? – was far more likely. Pyromania? Pyromaniacs usually – if one could ever use the word 'usually' when dealing with such unpredictable human behaviour – chose a far more accessible target, such as haystacks, barns, or crops. He drummed on the desk with his fingers. 'Then the case remains suspected arson and murder.'

'And if the lab finds traces of paraffin – subject to what the cook has to say – you can leave out the word suspected.'

•　　　•　　　•　　　•　　　•

Detective Sergeant Oliveland possessed many of the necessary attributes of a very successful detective except practical imagination and it was this lack which had prevented his gaining further promotion. He could successfully pursue all the threads of an investigation to the point where they led in one direction and then he lacked the imagination to believe it possible that the direction they indicated was not the correct one.

His manner, when questioning anyone, was kind and understanding and people were happy to confide in him. Within a couple of minutes of meeting Mrs. Barlowe in her hospital bed – she was now almost fully recovered – he had her chatting away as if they'd known each other a long time.

'I saw some of what she wore at night because she didn't mind walking around like that.'

'So what did Mrs. O'Reilly wear?'

'She'd pyjamas. Smart ones, some of 'em were.'

'Can you remember the colours and patterns?'

She thought back. 'I saw her in a red pair, with black

wriggly stripes. Then there was a black pair with thin gold and silver stripes.'

'Was that pattern anything like this?' Oliveland produced a small piece of material with charred edges.

'That's it, right enough ... Was that ... Was that what she was wearing?'

Oliveland returned the material to a plastic foam-filled container. Quickly and skilfully, he moved her mind on from that macabre relic. 'Tell me about all the valuable furniture. How was that looked after? What did you do to keep things like woodworm away?'

'Them! That was Vera's job and she was welcome to it! Mr. Pattison was always on about 'em. As I said to Vera more than once, if you ever find a live woodworm, you keep quiet or he'll have one of his tempers.'

'How did she treat the wood? Did she ever use ordinary paraffin?'

'Not likely, not with the stink that stuff makes. She'd a special polish.'

'One last thing and then I won't need to trouble you any more – when you checked up before going to bed, was everything as usual?'

'There wasn't nothing wrong or I'd have done something about it.'

'So all the paintings were hanging up in their usual places?'

'That they were. Used to frighten me, thinking how much they was worth.'

．　　　　．　　　　．　　　　．　　　　．

Crane hated post-mortems. He'd attended a large number, yet they never ceased to depress him. They pinpointed the unalterable march of death. You painfully gave up smoking to avoid lung cancer and you were promptly knocked down by a speeding car ...

'Never mind, Crane, it may never happen,' said the pathologist, as he crossed to the double wash-basin. He washed his gloved hands, then his bare hands. 'In all three cases, death was from asphyxiation or burning. Pattison was a sick man, though he probably didn't know it, and he hadn't all that long to live. Mrs. O'Reilly was two months' pregnant.' He took off his green overalls and handed them to the mortuary assistant, then looked at his watch. 'Good. I'll get back in time for supper.'

How in the hell could he look forward to supper? wondered Crane.

    •   •   •   •   •

Miles left Len's house, switched on the torch, and walked along the cinder path. He reached the road and turned right. Away on his left he saw a red glow in the sky which he immediately and with a touch of icy fear identified as a fire, but then he realized this was merely the reflection from the lights of the new garage in the village. It was going to be a long, long time before the thought of fire left him unmoved.

Car's headlights turned out of the priory drive and came along, harshly outlining him. When the car passed, he identified it as a police vehicle. Rumours that there was something funny about the fire were racing round the village. But surely no one could deliberately start a fire in which three persons burned to death?

He reached his house and went into the kitchen. He'd had lunch there and the dirty crockery and cutlery were still on the table. God! he thought, was there a surer or more dismal sign of a house without a woman in it than dirty washing-up lying around?

12

The Home Office safe expert finished burning a square through the strong-room door with the special oxy-acetylene equipment that could be adjusted to use up to ten thousand gallons of oxygen an hour. He picked up a seven-pound hammer and knocked in the central square of metal, standing well back in case the interior, despite all their care, had not cooled sufficiently and there was a burst of flames with the entry of fresh air. There were no flames.

The thinnest policeman present, dressed in overalls and wellingtons, crawled inside the strong-room and switched on a powerful torch. It was immediately clear that the strong-room, though old, had been fire-proof. There were seven locked jewel boxes, a locked metal cabinet, a large amount of silver plate, and a number of files. The silver and jewel boxes were handed out, the locked metal cabinet was gradually manhandled out, to the accompaniment of much cursing. The cabinet was opened by the Home Office expert and it contained a number of sculptured gold frogs, in various stances, with eyes of emerald and of superb workmanship, each packed in a shaped bed of polystyrene. Everything was checked, the inventory was signed by both Crane and Oliveland, and then it was all packed into a police van and driven to county H.Q.

    •   •   •   •   •

When Crane returned to his office late that afternoon, there was a note on his desk. Would he please ring Mr. James Hart, of Hart and Kleeper? He rang. The piece of canvas submitted for expert examination had proved to be between eighty and a hundred years old and in composition was exactly similar to the composition of French canvases of that period. One minute area of paintwork on the canvas had survived, though very considerably damaged, too considerably for any detailed and definitive examination. However, to experienced and expert eyes, the quality of the faintly discernible brushwork was quite definitely consistent with Pissarro's later and more mature work.

Crane thanked the didactic Mr. Hart and rang off. He began to doodle with a pencil. The strong-room hadn't been emptied and the paintings had been burned so that if the fire had been arson the most likely motive now was revenge on the part of an employee who knew the routine of the house.

    ·   ·   ·   ·

Miles was in the milk parlour, watching the first batch of cows go through. It was something he never tired of doing. There was a simple pleasure in watching the milk spurt into the five gallon jars, in time to the vacuum activated pulsator.

Andy took the clusters off the second cow on the right, hung them up, and checked the level of the milk. 'Up eight pounds. She's coming as good as her mother.' He pressed the control lever and the jar emptied rapidly.

'It's a pity her bag's unequal,' observed Miles.

'Doesn't mean a thing.'

Originally when they'd disagreed over a cow's potential, Andy had argued with resentful heat : now, he argued with good humour.

The door into the dairy slid open and Oliveland stepped

inside. He looked round, his thickset face showing surprise. 'It's like a bloomin' factory. If I was a cow, it'd scare me stupid.' He went to speak again and the trip-jar in the dairy started up the pump there and this had a high-pitched, grating sound that made conversation difficult even in the parlour. The noise ceased with the sharp click of a switch and the run-down of the pump. 'As I was going to say, before that row, could you give me five minutes?'

'O.K. Let's get out of here before this batch of cows are let out.'

Miles led the way through the dairy out on to the concrete drive.

Oliveland said: 'I need a bit of help – a little information. It's a question of how were things generally between your blokes and the boss and do you know anyone who might have had a grudge against him?'

'Against Mr. Pattison? Why d'you ask?'

'It's just we have to cover all sorts of questions.'

'Yeah?'

Oliveland scratched his right cheek. 'All right, we're looking for someone who could have had reason not to like him.'

'He wasn't a man anyone liked. But I suppose you mean something stronger? No, none of my blokes had any contact with him. Are you certain now, then, that it was arson?'

'What makes you think we ever thought that?'

'The village is thick with the story. And your men aren't searching every inch just for the hell of it. Surely to God, no one could have deliberately started that fire and burned three people to death?'

'If it was arson, the arsonist might not have reckoned on anyone getting trapped.'

'He must have seen the possibility.'

'If he'd a grudge, he may not have seen beyond his grudge.'

Miles took hold of the top rail of the post and rail fencing. If someone had deliberately set that fire . . .

'Well, many thanks for your help. If you should think of anything interesting, let one of us know.'

Oliveland said good-bye and left, walking down the drive. Miles watched him. The police believed the fire to have been arson. Yet to the ordinary person it seemed inconceivable that anyone would voluntarily set light to a house in which four people were known to be sleeping. Such a person would have to be a maniac. Yet the five men who worked on the farm were all normal, reasonable, humane persons, irritating and even stupid at times, yet undeniably sane.

     .   .   .   .   .

Crane knocked on the front door of the bungalow and when Simon opened the door, he introduced himself.

'Come along in, Inspector.' Then, because he was the man he was, Simon added: 'I'm afraid this place is very small, but we're having great trouble in finding an old, original farmhouse which is what my wife and I want.'

Crane stepped into the hall. It was a nice, ordinary, uninspired bungalow, the kind of place he hoped he'd be able to afford when he retired from the force and ceased to live in a police house. But he'd met many men like Simon and knew that if Simon had been living in a farmhouse, he'd have spoken about looking for a little Georgian mansion.

They went into the sitting-room, which was L-shaped with picture windows which looked out on to a fussily planned garden. Mrs. Simon was introduced. Tall, thin, and very vinegary, thought Crane. She left, to make them coffee.

'Now, to what do I owe the pleasure of your visit Inspector?'

'It's in connexion with the priory fire.'

'Quite terrible! It was a very dreadful shock to hear of the death of Mr. Pattison.'

Vera and Mrs. O'Reilly clearly didn't rate much sympathy. 'We've been making enquiries and there does seem to be a possibility that the fire was deliberate.'

'Good God!' But he didn't sound all that surprised.

'We're wondering if any of Mr. Pattison's farm employees had any cause to hold a grudge against him? Had there been any sort of trouble recently?'

An expression – almost of pleasure – crossed Simon's face. 'When you mention a grudge, you mean some reason for disliking Mr. Pattison, however unjustified? Well it does so happen, Inspector, I may be able to help you. You see Miles, the farm manager, was caught swindling Mr. Pattison and given a week's notice, to take effect as from Wednesday and . . . By God! The fire was that night.'

    •   •   •   •   •

Wesley Pace's overalls were white enough for any detergent advertisement: alongside him, Crane looked positively scruffy in overalls he'd borrowed from one of the P.C.s. They passed through a burned out doorway and came to a long pile of rubble in which searching had been going on until very recently stopped.

Pace pointed to a heap of fractured tiles which had fallen in such a manner as to form a small patch of cover. 'It's under there. Don't forget it's fragile.'

Crane first looked round himself. On his right was one of the outside walls, on his left an inner dividing wall with a chimney running up it. Where he stood had been the study and this was where one of the local firemen, first on the scene, claimed one of the seats of fire had been. Crane finally knelt down and Pace settled beside him. Pace indicated a three-inch length of charred wick. 'We're very lucky. It must first have survived the floor falling in and then the tiles came down to cover it completely.'

It was odd, thought Crane, how often evidence was preserved by what seemed to be divine intervention.

Pace said: 'A candle in the middle of inflammable material is one of the more popular time fuses. The candle burns down, ignites the material, which in turn ignites the room: it's almost foolproof if there's no great draught and it gives the arsonist plenty of time to escape. But once the inflammable material goes up the remaining length of candle is consumed very quickly and the wick sometimes gets preserved: it's because the wick is soaked in sulfate of ammonia which provides a surviving salt skeleton.

'Can the wick tell us anything?'

'Quite often, the laboratory can say what kind of a candle it came from. More than that, if there's any wood underneath on which candle grease dripped, that can be isolated and analysed and used in comparison tests.' Pace leaned back to sit on his heels. 'You've got yourself a case of arson.'

13

Miles was having breakfast on Monday morning when there was a knock on the kitchen door. When he shouted out to come in, Crane and Oliveland entered.

'Sorry to bother you yet again, Mr. Miles,' said Crane, 'but we've one or two more questions.'

'Could you manage a cup of coffee first?'

'That would go down a treat,' replied Oliveland.

Miles finished the last forkful of eggs and bacon before plugging in the electric kettle. 'Why not settle in the front room? It's more comfortable.'

He switched on the small electric fire for them, wondering vaguely why they were so silent, then returned to the kitchen and made three mugfuls of instant coffee which he put on a tray together with sugar and milk.

They helped themselves to milk and sugar – Oliveland clearly had a very sweet tooth – and Miles offered cigarettes. Crane refused one.

'Can you tell us anything more about the fire or about anyone who works here which might be of importance, Mr. Miles?' asked Crane.

Miles saw Oliveland open a notebook which he balanced on the arm of his chair. 'No, I can't. If I'd thought of anything, I'd've been in touch.'

'How did you happen to come to work here?'

He told them briefly.

'So Mr. Pattison owed you his life and when you came many years later to ask for his help he was happy to give you a job as farm manager?'

'Not quite,' corrected Miles. 'At first he said he couldn't help me personally, but he'd ask amongst his friends. I then had a letter to say he was sorry he couldn't do anything. It was only some time later that I got offered the job.'

'How did you get on as farm manager here? Any troubles?'

Something about Crane's tone of voice suddenly convinced Miles that the police had heard about the fertilizer. 'There was some trouble,' he admitted reluctantly. 'There was an argument over the amount of fertilizer that had been delivered.'

'And the upshot of this was you were given a week's notice?'

'Yes.'

'Yet when Sergeant Oliveland asked you if you knew of anyone who might hold a feeling of resentment against Mr. Pattison, why didn't you admit you did?'

Miles shrugged his shoulders. 'It was obvious your sergeant reckoned the answer could have a bearing on the fire. I knew that it didn't.'

'But you told him you'd heard rumours that arson was suspected. If it was arson, your sense of resentment surely was obviously relevant to the police, even if only for them to check it out and eliminate?'

'I had nothing to do with the fire. Christ! d'you think I could have set fire to the house, knowing Mrs. O'Reilly was asleep in it?'

'Couldn't you?' demanded Crane.

'Do I have to spell it out? I was in love with Anne and hoped to marry her.'

'The person who set the fire perhaps didn't intend to kill anyone.'

'It would have been obvious even to a half-wit that the terrible risk was there.'

'Had you known Mrs. O'Reilly for some little time?'

'Yes.'

'Were you aware she was two months' pregnant?'

Miles stared at Crane. 'You're lying,' he shouted.

'Her pregnancy was disclosed at the autopsy,' replied Crane, certain from Miles's reactions that he had not known this and that therefore his motive could not be revenge on her.

Miles's mind knew fresh, bleak bitterness. Anne's pregnancy explained her strange behaviour. Yet if only she'd told him. He would have ... Even in such despair, he was self-honest enough to wonder whether their relationship could have remained the same if he'd known that she'd been having an affair with another man while friendly with him?

'I'm sorry to have had to tell you that ... What time did you go to bed Wednesday night?'

'How the hell do I know?'

'Was it early or late?'

'Early. I was watching the television and every programme was tripe.'

'Did you leave the house at all during the night?'

'Only when I woke up and saw the priory was on fire.'

'What woke you?'

'Shouting.'

'Who was shouting?'

'I don't know.'

Crane rubbed the side of his thin nose. 'Have you any objection to us making a quick search of this house?'

'Search for what?'

'For anything which might help our investigations.'

'You need a warrant for that.'

'Only if you refuse us permission. If you've nothing to hide, why refuse us?'

'For all I care, you can turn the place inside out.'

'Thank you.' Crane stood up, nodded at Oliveland, and

left the room. Oliveland slipped the notebook into his coat pocket and followed Crane.

The bastards, thought Miles wildly. There'd been a fire, he had cause for resentment against Pattison, so they made him a suspect for arson and murder. No matter that he'd been in love with Anne ...

They returned and Oliveland held a round china pot in which were four ordinary white household candles. Crane said: 'These were in the larder. Are they yours?'

'Are they likely to be someone else's if they're in my larder?'

'I'm going to take them away. I'll give you a receipt for them.'

'To hell with receipts.'

Crane carefully wrote out a receipt, taking a copy with carbon paper. He tore off the top copy and handed it to Miles, who scrumpled it up and threw it into the fireplace. Crane's expression didn't alter. He brought a plastic bag from his pocket, put the four candles in it, added a piece of paper on which he wrote the date, place, and time, and signed his initials. 'Where did you buy them?'

'At the local store.'

'When?'

'How can I remember a thing like that? I just bought them.'

'Did you originally buy more than four?'

'I don't remember.'

Crane formally said good-bye and left. Oliveland said nothing and the last look he gave Miles was one of questioning dislike.

Miles stayed slumped in the chair. Why couldn't Anne have told him?

    •   •   •   •   •

Crane and Oliveland sat in the front of Crane's car which was still parked.

'You didn't push him very hard,' said Oliveland, with the easy familiarity of a man who'd been a detective sergeant for a long time. 'He's beginning to look a natural.'

'But he didn't know she was knocked up.'

Oliveland shrugged his shoulders. Didn't he see the possible significance of that? wondered Crane. It was odd how often the detective sergeant ignored human emotions: but then he was of the old school — 'Who's the natural? Then he's our lad, no matter how bloody clever he's been. Where's the local store?'

'Straight on down to the T junction and turn right.'

The village was sited on cross-roads and Crane stopped the car outside the general store. 'Go in and find out what you can.'

When Oliveland returned, he opened the passenger door and sat down and then, typically, said nothing but waited to be asked.

'Well?' snapped Crane.

'He bought half a dozen candles soon after starting work here.'

'So he's used two. And there were possibly two seats of fire . . . Did you think to ask if there've been any power cuts since he bought them?'

'Naturally. There hasn't been a power cut in over nine months.'

•   •   •   •   •

Simon drove a Vauxhall, four years old, which he unfailingly polished once a week. To anyone who'd listen he'd explain that he hadn't bought a new car because his particular model was the best the firm had produced for a very long time. He parked in front of the gate of

Miles's house and climbed out. He nervously fiddled with the white handkerchief in the breast pocket of his blazer and vainly wished he'd refused to do as the detective inspector had asked.

Squaring his shoulders, he walked round the house to the kitchen door, knocked on this, and went straight in. As agent to the estate, he didn't wait to be invited in.

Miles, who was opening a can of baked beans, looked up with sharp annoyance, but didn't immediately say anything.

'Getting ready for lunch, then?' Even Simon recognized the fatuity of that remark.

Miles emptied the contents of the can into a saucepan. 'Is there something you want?'

'Yes, there is. Today's Tuesday.'

'So I believe.' Miles's voice was sarcastic.

'Your . . . your notice was for a week and so your employment officially ends tomorrow.'

Miles switched on the larger of the rings.

'I was wondering if, in the circumstances . . . The truth is . . . Look, I did what I could to persuade Mr. Pattison not to sack you. As I told him, agriculture isn't a high wage industry and people have always made a little on the side. Your real trouble was, you just made a little too much.' He plucked his handkerchief from the breast pocket of his blazer and brushed it along his lips. 'Of course, Mr. Pattison was . . . *De mortuis nil nisi bonum* and all that . . . He was a very hard man. If the matter had been left to me, I would merely have issued a reprimand.'

'As a matter of interest, how much would I have had to pinch before you'd have agreed to sack me?'

Simon ignored the question. 'Everything's in a state of turmoil now, but the estate has to be looked after until

113

the lawyers are finished. So what I've come to say is, will you stay on as farm manager? You've improved things so much in the short time you've been here. Quite extraordinary, the difference.'

'So what happens over the fertilizer?'

'That will be all forgotten.'

'Not by the police.'

'I shall inform them there was no certainty as to what happened : no proof.'

'Will you sign a statement to that effect?'

'I ... Yes. Yes, I will.'

'Give me the statement, then I'll stay on as farm manager.'

'Excellent. Capital. And I shall strongly advise whoever is the new owner of the estate to continue your employment. Then that's settled. Good morning, Miles.'

As Simon left, Miles put the saucepan on the ring, which he turned down because it was now red hot. The bloody fool, he thought, to imagine his story could be believed. He'd been overjoyed to have the chance to sack Miles. So why not have the guts to admit the truth that the death of Pattison had so upset everything that he'd not got around to hiring another farm manager in time .... Miles drew in his breath sharply. Now he was being the bloody fool. Simon wouldn't have denied himself the chance of getting rid of someone he disliked because the farm might suffer. He must have been persuaded to ask Miles to stay on. And the only people who would have done that were the police. And their only motive could be that they wanted to keep their suspect under close observation.

Until now, he had known only disgusted, shocked, resentment that the detective inspector could be so warped in mind as to believe he could have set the fire in which

Anne had died. But he realized that he should also have been afraid. The police had been suspicious from the beginning that the fire was not accidental and they'd been searching for a man with a reason for hating Pattison: they thought they'd found him. They had taken away four candles. Four? But he'd bought six and not used any. So where were the other two?

The beans began to bubble and he moved the saucepan off the ring. He turned and walked into the larder. The top shelf was just not too high for him to be able to look along it. There were no candles left behind: only some dirty paper, a cracked plate, and a lot of dust.

•   •   •   •   •

Sifting the rubble hour after hour was a job that called for endless patience. Police Constable Younger was no fool, but he did have the ability to carry out the most repetitive of jobs with a happy indifference to boredom. Even after eight days of searching through the rubble he still worked with the same care and attention as on the first day. Part of his mind was usually devoted to thinking about his fiancée: had he had more imagination – in which case the job would have seemed far more onerous – he might have realized that she would come, when older, to resemble her mother more closely and his thoughts then would not have been so pleasant.

He found the metal object at a quarter to eleven on Friday morning, in what had been the breakfast-room. He picked it up and held it in the palm of his right hand. Clearly some sort of a badge, heat had warped it so that now it was impossible to visualize its original shape. He called the sergeant over.

The sergeant scrambled across. 'What have you got for us this time, Sammy?'

'Search me, Sarge. Some kind of badge, that's all I can say.'

The sergeant took it and examined it. He brought a small plastic bag from his pocket and dropped the badge into this, adding a note of position, date, and time, and his initials. Then, on a scale plan, he marked the exact spot where it had been found.

.　　　　.　　　　.　　　　.　　　　.

The laboratory technician looked at the warped and twisted badge, then at the electric clock above one of the far benches. Eleven o'clock on a Saturday morning. In any civilized job, one was at home at such a time. Resentfully, he clamped the badge into a small vice, fixed up a screen of white cardboard, and shone a torch to throw the shadow of the badge on to the screen. The shadows failed to merge into any recognizable pattern.

He used a very sharp knife to nick an edge of the metal and after examination through a powerful magnifying glass he decided to bend the metal back to its original shape. He used a gas fed pencil burner to heat a corner of the badge and tested the metal constantly with powerful tweezers. After some time, the metal became pliable.

Because he worked with such painstaking care, it took him nearly three-quarters of an hour to straighten out the badge to a reasonable degree and even now there was still too much distortion for him to make out its identity. He drew – he was no mean artist – the present shape on to a thin piece of rubber, cut this out, and stretched it in different directions. Two letters, M and N, took shape.

Using heat on the badge again, he worked the metal until he had reconstructed an M and an N. This restored some semblance of shape to the remainder of the badge. Above the central letters there was a small crown and the outer sides were composed of clustered leaves.

•   •   •   •   •

Miles walked the paddock and noticed how the indigenous rye grasses were taking over from the weed grasses. Pundits said it took two or three years to restore a field, but in just a few months there was a sharp response to draining and a heavy winter dressing of basic slag.

He heard the caw of a crow and looked up. It was circling the old priory. To the right he could just make out through the trees – the leaves of some had browned and died – the stark smoke-blackened walls of the new priory.

The farm offered bitter memories and perhaps he should have scorned Simon's offer to stay on. Yet, even while it hurt, when he walked the fields and saw the improvements it also offered him a consoling affirmation that life was not useless.

An early covey of partridges flushed, the five youngsters very small. He watched them and saw them pitch down about a clump of stinging nettles which had somehow escaped being sprayed so he made a circular detour to avoid flushing them a second time. He passed through a gate on to the road. A quarter of a mile up the road, parked by his house, was a car he recognized. Crane's. What did the bastard want now?

'I've some more questions,' said Crane. 'Shall we go inside your place?'

'If you like,' he answered curtly.

Crane and Oliveland followed Miles round to the kitchen and then through to the front room. Crane began asking questions as soon as they were seated and Olive-land took notes.

'When were you at sea?'

'During the latter part of World War Two and for a few years afterwards.'

'In what?'

'The Merchant Navy.'

'When you came for the interview with Mr. Pattison, where did you go in the house?'

'I was shown into the large sitting-rooom.'

'Once you'd started working here, did Mr. Pattison invite you to the house at any time?'

'No.'

'I suppose you must have resented that a little?'

'Why should I? I was an employee, not a bosom friend.'

'But you'd saved his life.'

'A debt he judged he'd repaid in full when he employed me.'

'You sound bitter?'

'I didn't intend to.'

'After your first visit, did you ever again go into any of the public rooms?'

'No.'

'Or the bedrooms?'

'Of course not.'

'You never entered the breakfast-room?'

'I've already said I've only ever been in the large sitting-room.'

'During the war, what did you wear on leave?'

Miles stared blankly at the detective inspector, bewildered by this abrupt change in the conversation.

'Did you wear uniform or civvies?'

'Civvies, after I'd got over the boyish pride of uniform.'

'Wasn't that a bit tricky? In war time people get very jingoistic and think anyone in civvies of service age is a shirker. Or did you wear some sort of emblem to show you were in the Merchant Navy?'

'What in the name of hell does that matter?'

'It matters. Did you wear any kind of an emblem?'

'We used to have a badge in our lapels.'

'What kind of a badge?'

'It was silver coloured and had M.N. on it.'

'Have you still got yours?'

'It's somewhere around.' Miles shrugged his shoulders.

'Would you see if you can find it?'

Miles stood up and left the room. He went up the stairs and along to his bedroom.

He kept the badge, along with a small sliver of wood from the gunwale of the lifeboat they'd been rescued in, in a small tobacco tin covered with an intricate pattern in leather which he'd bought in Mombasa. He opened the tin. The sliver of wood was there but there was no silver coloured lapel badge. He lifted up the cotton wool and shook it. Then, the haste of growing panic in his actions, he searched the drawer the tin had been in and the remaining four drawers of the old and battered chest-of-drawers.

When he returned downstairs, he tried to speak in a normal tone, but his voice was hoarse. 'It's not there.'

Crane's expression didn't change : his voice remained even. 'When did you last see it?'

'I can't remember.'

Crane took a plastic container from his pocket, removed the lid, and showed Miles the contents. Miles saw a blackened and distorted M.N. badge. There could be no certainty this was his, yet he didn't doubt it was, nor that it had been found in the ruins of the priory.

'Someone's taken it,' he said violently.

'Why should anyone break into your house and take it?'

The words came in a wild rush. 'To try and frame me for the fire.'

'Why should anyone try to do that?'

'How would I know?'

'Who would hate you enough to frame you for the murder of three people?'

'I've just said, I don't know.'

'Then doesn't it seem rather unlikely.'

'Can't you begin to understand? Nothing on God's earth would have made me do anything that might have harmed Anne.'

Crane stared at Miles, a slight frown creasing his forehead. Then he stood up. 'I shall need to question you again after certain results have come through from the forensic lab.' He turned and walked to the door. Oliveland slowly followed him.

Miles stared at the newly shut door. Because he knew that the truth was that he had not set the fire, he also knew that whoever had set it had faked the evidence to make it seem he was guilty. Who? Why?

14

Andy Stoddard, like so many cowmen, was slow of speech, conservative of thought, but far from stupid, and careful of movement. By way of sharp contrast, his wife was a hoppity sparrow of a woman, never happy unless doing something. There had been considerable edge between Andy and Miles until Stoddard decided that Miles was nearly as good a cowman as himself, then a working relationship had grown up between them which had become something only slightly less than friendship after the fire. Yet, when Miles went to his house for supper on the Sunday, he almost immediately became aware of his and his wife's uneasiness.

'Looks like rain, maybe,' said Andy, after a long silence.

'I think you're right,' answered Miles.

'The grass ain't needing any for a while. The new lay's coming up well in the five-acre.'

'It's been a very good take,' agreed Miles.

Andy ran a forefinger round inside the open collar of his shirt, as if finding the atmosphere oppressive. He rolled himself a cigarette. Mrs. Stoddard was darning a sock. Usually, she talked incessantly, yet tonight she had hardly spoken.

Andy licked the edge of the cigarette paper and stuck it down. 'Milk was up a few pounds.'

'Let's hope it keeps going in that direction.' They had learned the police suspected him, thought Miles, and were desperately uncomfortable over having him in the house.

Andy lit his cigarette. He searched around for something to say. 'The driver of the milk lorry reckons the price of milk'll have to go up soon.'

'I'll believe that when it happens. The government couldn't care less about a reasonable profit on capital invested.'

'I must be getting supper,' said Mrs. Stoddard suddenly, in her thin, high-pitched voice. 'I'm afraid it's only stew and bread and cheese, Harry.'

He decided to cut short this painful visit. 'I've started

up a hell of a headache. Would you mind too much if I don't stay?'

'Can't you just have a quick bite with us first?' she asked, bravely trying to make out that they hoped he'd stay.

'Thanks a lot, Madge, but it's a real pounder and I'll get straight to bed.'

He said good-bye, switched on his torch, and left. As he walked down the cinder path he thought, with a growing bitterness, that even out in the country, where things happened quietly and men were slow to make up their minds, suspicion fast became certainty.

He turned on to the road. From a copse came the eerie scream of a vixen, from nearer the hoot of a tawny owl. The wind rustled the leaves of the hedgerow ashes and oaks. A bulling cow began to blare with the monotonous regularity that was so exasperating except to bulls. Sounds of the countryside. Sounds which he had lived with throughout his life except when he'd been at sea. If the police became quite certain of his guilt and he was tried, convicted, and imprisoned . . . Goddamn it, he thought with frightened anger, now he was assuming his own conviction. But he hadn't started that fire, so no one could ever prove that he had. Anyone with the slightest common sense would know he couldn't have risked Anne's life . . . Yet the police had a great deal of common sense and they plainly believed he had. And the evidence they kept uncovering said he had . . .

He reached the house and went in. He was pouring himself out a gin when the telephone rang and he walked through to the front room.

'Is that Mr. Miles?' asked a man.

The voice was soft and syrupy, the kind of voice which Miles disliked on hearing. 'Yes.'

'You don't know me, which I'm sure is a very great pity, but I've something very important to tell you. Come up to London without telling anyone tomorrow and be outside gate number six at Charing Cross station at eight o'clock in the evening. Have you got all that?'

'Who the hell are you?'

'Eight o'clock, gate number six.' The connexion was cut.

He slowly replaced the receiver. If that hadn't been a pointless hoax, it had to have some sort of connexion with the priory tragedy.

．　　　．　　　．　　　．　　　．

'British Railways!' said the man who sat opposite his wife in the railway compartment. 'You can set your watch by 'em, just as the advert says. Provided you like your watch dead slow.'

'I expect we're late because they're laying the new line, dear,' she answered.

Miles looked at his watch. They were almost at Victoria now and they were over half-an-hour behind schedule. It was odds on the man who'd made the telephone call the previous night would not have waited. Disgruntled, he began to wonder why he'd ever bothered to come up.

The train entered the station and drew up at its platform. Miles left the carriage, hurried along the platform, and went out to the taxi rank. Because it had begun to drizzle, after a day of overcast skies, a lot of other people were also waiting for taxis and the supply was low. The queue moved slowly and it was another ten minutes before he climbed into the back seat of a taxi after telling the driver to go to Charing Cross. It would have been far quicker and cheaper, he thought, even more disgruntled, to have gone by tube.

At Charing Cross he paid off the cab and went through the main entrance and booking hall into the square which was still thronged with people. He checked where number six platform was, crossed to the gate and stood there for several minutes. Then, tiredly, he walked the few yards to the bookstall and stared at the magazines.

'I . . . I thought you weren't coming, Harry,' she said.

He turned, certain his brain was tricking him. Anne was dead.

15

The meal was English. The eggs were over-cooked, the half bottle of Beaune had surely started life close to Algeria, the coffee was bitter, the staff were feeling as resentful as they looked and, by banging everything that could reasonably be banged, made it clear that although they were paid to work late, late customers were a damned nuisance.

'How?' Miles stared across the table at her, noticing fresh grey hairs amongst her tight black curls, the fact that her eyes were even bluer than he had remembered them, that her snub nose added a carefree hint to a face which was otherwise looking drawn, that she was not young yet there was an essential youthfulness about her. 'How?' He spoke almost harshly. 'I've been torturing myself over your death. When I stood outside the priory as it was burning and tried to believe you weren't in it, whilst in my heart was certain you must be . . .' He became silent.

She spoke in a whisper. 'You've got to try to understand . . . Oh, God, you're going to hate me.'

He saw the tears in her eyes and reached across the table to put his hand on hers. 'Hate you? Don't you know even now that I love you?'

She looked even sadder. 'If only I'd known you . . .' She told him about her life.

.   .   .   .   .

Her name was Mary Walsh. Her father had always disliked children and when her mother had discovered she was pregnant, she'd desperately tried to have an abortion. With legal abortions then virtually unobtainable for a healthy, poor woman, she'd gone to a back-street abortionist. The abortion was clumsily carried out, very painful, and unsuccessful.

Her father, too old to be called up, had stayed for a while – home was a small flat, just not in slums – but then he'd met a woman twelve years younger than his wife, who had no screaming children, did not spend much of her time ill, enjoyed sex, and had been left some money by a husband killed in Tobruk.

Her mother had blamed her for her father's departure. If she hadn't arrived, he would still be at home, her mother wouldn't feel ill, there would be money in the house, and everything in the garden would be lovely. Her feeling of guilt – she was far too young to realize its cruelly false base – became so great that she tried to commit suicide.

Officialdom was, of course, shocked. How could a child be so wicked/mentally unbalanced/stupid as to try to kill herself. Her mother had wept and explained that her daughter had always been difficult, so difficult in fact that she'd driven her father out of the house. She was beyond control. So officialdom looked after her. They were kind, by their standards, and they sincerely tried to help her, but it was still war time and trained staff were at a premium.

What she most clearly remembered about the first home they kept her in was the further sense of guilt she suffered because she could not like the staff as much as the staff said she should, the clothes which were all hand-me-downs, the prayers which asked that she be made a better girl and not that the world should be made a better place for her, and the awful sick feeling when parents came to visit the other girls and her mother didn't. Her mother wrote a few letters but then these stopped. She wrote each Sunday, by order, and after the first five months each letter was returned with the notation that the addressee was gone from the given address and had not left a forwarding one.

When she was twelve she went to a home where the staff, mostly newly returned from the war, had been fully trained. They had tried to repair the damage which had been done, but were largely too late. She had learned that no one wanted her, not even her own mother, that men were viciously selfish, that charity was even colder than popularly supposed, and that in a harsh world one had to fight with no holds barred for anything and everything.

They trained her for life, in so far as they could afford to : they taught her a little typing, a little sewing, and a little cooking.

Her first job was as a junior clerk in a solicitor's office. The firm specialized in divorce and much of the evidence in the defended divorce cases reinforced her contemptuous hatred for men. A hatred that was suddenly called in doubt when one of the partners began to show her the kind of kindness she had never before enjoyed. He took her out to the theatre, orchestral concerts, art exhibitions, restaurants, and showed her a whole new side to life. He taught her that there was laughter and fun and happiness everywhere and that people should enjoy themselves. He seduced her without trouble, or much skill, frequently promised to marry her but found many legal precepts and precedents to explain why their friendship would have to cease when she became eighteen and pregnant. He was not a rotter, though: he arranged and even paid for an abortion which was neatly, clinically, and effectively carried out.

The next years of her life were not ones she cared to remember too closely. Bitterness, hatred, a yearning she refused to acknowlege, the need to revenge herself, led her into a wild, careless life. She'd met a T.V. producer who'd fed her on the old corn that she could act, he could get her jobs, and where was the nearest bed. Funnily enough, she discovered she could act. Never well enough to make much of a career, but enough to get some work. Inevitably, she made contact with the outer fringes of the criminal world and she enjoyed those contacts. Many criminals seemed to have much the same outlook on life as she did.

Only Oliver fascinated her for any length of time, and this even after she had come to understand that he was vicious but weak, amoral, and a coward. He made occasional use of her in his criminal activities, which were always those of a man too scared ever to take a direct risk. He enjoyed the favours of a steady stream of women because there was something about him which appealed to the latent masochism in every woman. She finally reached her limit, and was about to leave him when he told her of a job he'd got.

Go down into the country and live it rich, get some moon-faced rustic to fall for her, lead him into bed, tell him a tear-plucking story which would relieve him of a few centuries, pocket the cash and another five centuries for her trouble, and return to the Big Smoke and fun. Make money and a fool out of a man? Yes.

She hadn't liked Pattison. But he'd been polite and he hadn't stormed her bed. She'd waited a while before making contact with the bucolic mug and during this time she'd been surprised, even shocked, to discover that there was something about the countryside which answered a need within her soul. There was peace, a sense of continuity, meaningful values . . .

Harry Miles was not the man she had expected. He didn't try and rush her behind a hay-stack. He wasn't bucolic. He'd been to places she'd only read about, spent years around the Mediterranean learning to live with himself, which was something she'd never managed. He'd suffered heartbreaks, but had overcome them by strength of character.

The fake attack in the road had been well planned and cleverly executed. Its immediate effect had been to set up the relationship between them, but its longer term effect had been to make her question what she was doing.

Determined not to let a second man fool her, she'd gone ahead with the plans. When the time was right, she'd offered bed, knowing there wasn't a man alive who could refuse sex when it was offered cleverly enough to make him believe he'd done all the running. Only Harry Miles had refused to run true to form and he'd turned down sex with words of love.

She'd always thought of herself as mentally tough. Yet a few words of genuine love, which made her recognize the truth that she loved him, and she became like the

128

seventeen-year-old who'd seen stars in her solicitor lover's eyes. She'd almost told Harry as much as she knew of what was happening to him. In bed that night, she'd cried for what might have been.

What to do? Desperate for help, there'd be no one to offer it. Oliver, if he learned she was lousing up her job, would have her beaten up stupid: Harry would hate her for what she had been. And what was it she had become mixed up in? Why had she been sent down to seduce a farm manager who couldn't be of any importance in a world which measured importance by wealth and power?

Then she'd read about the death of Señor Miguel Luque. The report made it appear he had accidentally become tangled up with a terrorist's bomb. Accidentally? Like hell. Terrified, she'd fled Breakthorn Priory. And two days later she'd learned about the fire and the finding of the body which had been identified as hers and she'd known that, as terrified as she had been, she should have been much more terrified.

The days had passed and the papers had made it clear, if one had the wit to read between the lines, that arson was suspected, that the three dead people had been murdered, and that the police had their suspicions who were guilty. Then, to her increased horror, it became obvious that their suspicions were centred on Harry.

She could have kept quiet about her existence and have continued to hide out from the mob who'd organized the job and who must be tearing the place apart to find and kill her. But she persuaded an old friend of hers – a harmless queer – to telephone and arrange the meeting at Charing Cross. She'd arrived at seven-thirty, terror and love making her feel sick. Time had passed. He'd been arrested. He'd just not bothered to come. In the bar, she'd had several drinks, leaving from time to time to cross the hall to see if by some miracle he was now waiting by platform number six. Then she'd made the last journey, finally convinced he was not coming. . . .

· · · · ·

She stubbed out a cigarette. 'So now you've just a little of the muddy picture, Harry.'

He stared at her, a tight expression on his face.

'I . . .' She paused, then spoke in a rush. 'I had to tell you. I wanted you to try and understand. Except there's no real understanding. Oh, Christ! If only I could have met someone like you at the beginning. . . .'

'Shut up,' he said harshly.

She gulped. Somehow, she'd fooled herself into believing that when he learned about her childhood he might be able to accept how it had all happened, how she had given herself to men for whom she felt only contempt and whom she delighted in humiliating, how she'd stayed with Oliver even whilst she despised him, how she had come to travel south to fool a moon-faced rustic.

One of the waitresses, middle-aged, tired, came across. 'It's late, you know. Some of us wants to get home.'

Silently, he picked up the bill, pushed back the chair, and walked along to the cash desk where he paid.

Anne, tears blurring her eyes, followed him.

He pocketed the change and left, holding the swing door open for her. Four people, two couples arm-in-arm, passed and then the pavement was clear. He faced her. 'Where are you staying?'

'You don't have to bother . . .'

'Where are you staying?'

'In a tiny flat half a mile away,' she replied, in a whisper. 'The queer owns it and is letting me stay there.'

'Let's get moving.'

She stared at him, momentarily frightened she was reading far more into his words than was there. But then she saw the look in his eyes and knew that she wasn't.

·　　　·　　　·　　　·　　　·

The bed was small, the mattress was very old, very lumpy, it sagged in the middle, and they didn't give a damn. They made love with desperate need and wild abandon that jetted them into a different world.

Afterwards, when she stroked his back, she said : 'I love you.'

He rolled over and kissed her. He ran his hand down her body, noticing how the first marks of approaching middle age were settling so that the flesh around her stomach had slackened. He leaned over to kiss that slack flesh. 'And I love you.'

'Say that again and again. Tell me you'll never let me go.'

'I love you. I'll never let you go.'

'That's only once. Say it again.'

'Marry me.'

'Harry !' She pressed her body fiercely and possessively against his.

'Well?'

'Well what?'

'Will you marry me?'

'Don't say that. Just keep saying you love me.'

'Why?'

'Because.'

'Because what?'

'Harry, Harry. I told you.'

'What did you tell me?'

'That I'm ... That I was ...'

'Little fool. There is no past.'

'There has to be.'

'Not for us. I love you and that is now. When I was bumming my way around the Mediterranean, I learned that the only thing which really matters in life is life now. Do you love me?'

'More than is possible.'

'Then we get married.'

'But you once told me you divided women into those you slept with and those you married.'

'You form a unique and third category. Even my talking-to-God father would agree on that.'

Because her head was pressed against his and her tight black curls were on his cheeks, he couldn't see her face. 'What's the matter?' he asked.

'I'm crying.'

'Stop crying. A tear's dribbling down my chest and it's cold and wet.'

She kissed him with wild violence and his arms closed round her.

No one, he said later, would have believed they were getting on in years.

16

The one-bedroomed flat was cheaply furnished and it overlooked either a drab, grey street or a back yard which looked as if it had become a communal rubbish dump.

Miles was sitting at the small table which just fitted between the stove and the door. 'Anne . . .' He stopped.

She realized why he'd stopped. 'Harry, go on calling me Anne. Mary Walsh has vanished.' She left the stove, turned, bent down and kissed him. He held her close to himself.

'Let me go, Harry, or the eggs will burn.' She laughed, kissed him again, and then pulled free. She finished cooking the eggs, bacon, and fried bread, dished them up, and carried the plates to the table.

'I shouldn't be eating like this, Harry,' she said, as she sat down. 'I'm overweight as it is.'

'So I noticed.'

'Swine!'

He smiled. 'But I've always liked plump women, they're so much more friendly . . . We must find out how soon we can get married. Aren't there things like special licences?'

She fiddled with her fork, prodding a piece of fried bread.

'What's the matter now?' he asked quietly.

She laid the fork down on the plate. 'I . . . I don't think I want to marry you, Harry. Let's just play it as you said – all that there is is today. Tomorrow's a different world.'

He interrrupted her halting words. 'Look at me.'

Reluctantly, she looked up.

'Now tell me, eyeball to eyeball, that you don't want to marry me, the most handsome man in sight.'

She reached across the table and gripped his hand. 'I'm terrified for you,' she answered in a whisper. 'If you stay with me, they'll try to kill you.'

'Who are they?'

She shook her head. 'I don't know. From the moment I read about the woman who was supposed to be me, being burned to death . . .'

133

'Oliver told you nothing?'

'Only what I was to do down at the priory.'

'Would he know all the facts?'

'No.' She spoke without hesitation. 'He's just a contact man, pimp, and banker.'

'But he told you to work with Pattison. So he must know a certain amount of what went on?'

'Not enough to help us.'

'You took fright when you heard about the death of Luque, who'd been cleaning the paintings?'

'Yes. I knew it couldn't be a genuine accident because of all the circumstances.'

'What in the hell was Pattison up to? Why get you to persuade me to swindle him out of a few hundred pounds?' He became silent and finished eating. He asked her whether she'd like more coffee and when she refused he poured himself out a cupful. All the time he was away from the table, she watched him as if scared he would suddenly disappear.

'The answer to the second question has to be, Anne, that he wanted a reason for sacking me because then I'd have a motive for setting the fire . . . The whole set-up was geared to make me resentful: for instance, how he'd praise me for the way I was managing the place and then almost immediately he'd make certain that that old fool Simon reprimanded me for something obviously stupid. The more resentful I became, the more ready I'd be to try and swindle him – especially to help someone I'd fallen in love with. Look at the way you had to tell me you'd asked Pattison for a small loan and he'd refused, a man who could have lent you a hundred times as much without worry . . . So why all this?'

She offered him a pack of cigarettes and they both smoked.

'There were several reports in the papers that he was in some sort of financial trouble,' he said slowly. 'Suppose the reports were accurate. We know Luque was in the house cleaning paintings worth over a million quid and Luque was almost certainly murdered . . .' He shook his head.

'What, Harry?'

'There's something wrong. I'm sure Pattison had some sort of complicated scheme set up, with me directly involved in case something went wrong. Probably it was a scheme cooked up with the expert help of one of the prisoners in the jail where he was a prison visitor. But Luque was killed and Pattison would never have envisaged murder. A swindle, yes. But murder's something very different and it couldn't be in his character.

'His scheme must have been to raise money, mustn't it? And must have concerned Luque. . . . Did you ever go into the room Luque was using?'

She shook her head. 'No. We had very strict orders to keep out of it.'

'Why should Pattison have brought a picture-cleaner all the way from Spain? After all, some of the world's best experts at cleaning and restoring paintings are in England.'

'Could they have wanted to charge too much? Pattison watched every penny he spent.'

'Isn't it far more likely it was because Luque hardly spoke English? So when he'd finished his job, he'd return to Spain and would never hear . . .' He stopped.

'Hear what?'

'About the fire which burned the five paintings.' His voice quickened. 'Anne, that has to be it. The paintings were to appear to burn, so the insurance money could be collected. But it was an insurance swindle that was in layers. When there's a fire which destroys something valuable that's insured, the police and insurers automatically investigate the possibility of a swindle. Proof of arson, naturally, turns any suspicion into certainty. Pattison, or his jail adviser, knew this. So they designed the swindle in layers. The first layer concerned the paintings. It was no good just removing them before the fire. Their absence could be remarked in one of a dozen ways. So Luque was brought over to England to forge as near perfect copies as he could. When the fifth and last one was completed, the originals were all shipped away. In the meantime, layer two was underway. Everything would be done to make the fire seem accidental, but forensic investigation can often prove a so-called accidental fire was in reality arson. So they decided that if the police became reasonably certain it was arson, there would be evidence at hand to suggest a motive very far removed from any insurance swindle – in other words, that's where I came in as the fall guy. And added to this, any traces of the painting left by the fire would appear to be genuine, helping to refute the swindle theory. . . . That was the way Pattison meant to play it. But.'

'But what?'

'There must have been layer number three, only Pattison never knew this. His was a straightforward insurance swindle, but his adviser wasn't content to settle for just a cut in the rewards, he wanted the lot. So he let Pattison go ahead, but then at the crucial moment took over. He murdered Pattison in the fire because it made the discovery of the swindle much less likely, yet at the same time it then didn't even matter to him if the police did uncover layer number two. He'd have the million pounds' worth of paintings.

'They – the original adviser and whoever he had work-

136

ing with him – killed Luque because, unlike Pattison, they were realists. They knew that the only man who can be guaranteed not to talk is the dead man. With him dead, in what was apparently an accident, they were safe. Or they would have been if you hadn't read about the "accident" and taken fright. You, after all, were also due to die in the fire.'

She stubbed out her cigarette with hands that shook.

'When you disappeared, they were in trouble. If there was the arranged fire and you were missing, the police would want to know why. They'd begin to investigate your history and they'd find . . .' He stopped.

'They'd find,' she said bitterly, 'that I'd got the kind of past that would raise suspicions.'

'So someone had to die in your place. It was because of this unknown woman, chosen to resemble you as closely as possible, that there had to be two sources of fire to make certain she was burned to the point where she could not be facially recognized. Ironically, it was the presence of two sources of fire which first made certain arson was suspected.'

'How . . . how could they have made certain Pattison and the woman stayed in the house when it was on fire? Did they drug them?'

'I doubt it. Drugs could have been discovered in the post-mortems. In any case, how to get them to take a drug without suspecting?'

'Then what?'

'A person can be knocked unconscious by an expert and there'll be only slight bruising which'll burn away in a fire or be put down to something falling on to that person. It's my guess their arms and legs were tied with cotton, soaked in something so that it would burn right away when the fire reached them.'

137

She was horrified by the picture. 'If the paper hadn't bothered to print that brief mention of Luque's death – and this simply because he'd just been in England – or I'd missed the mention...'

'You'd have died in that fire as I thought you had.'

'But . . . but some other woman would have lived.' After a moment she said : 'What do we do now?'

'Tell the police everything we know or suspect.'

'Harry . . . you haven't quite worked things out, have you? Most of what you've said can't be proved. You keep talking about the men behind Pattison. What if the police never discover who they were? And . . . and don't you see that all the time I'm alive I'm a threat to the mob because as far as they're concerned I might know something to help identify them. If the police know I'm alive, the press will get hold of the story...'

He imagined faceless men searching for her. 'How safe are you here?'

She looked blankly at him.

'Where did you meet the man who owns this flat?'

'In the pub where he always goes – it's full of other queers.'

'Could they trace you through meeting him there?'

For a second she looked worried, then she shook her head. 'I was only in there for roughly a quarter of an hour. Anyway, how could anyone who saw me have known who I was?'

He relaxed. She was right.

She broke the ensuing silence. 'What are we going to do, Harry?'

He smiled to reassure her. 'Sit back and do nothing. The Spanish have a saying : "Let your troubles wait : in the end they'll get so bored they'll go away".'

·   ·   ·   ·   ·

Crane drove along from the cross-roads to the farm drive and parked. He climbed out and briefly looked up at the sky : there was hardly a cloud in sight and the sun was warm. It reminded him that he had rashly promised his wife a holiday this year, come what may.

Detective Constable Retson came round the side of Miles's house, opened the gate, and stepped out. 'There's been no sign of him all day, sir.'

'Have you checked whether anyone on the farm knows anything?'

'Yes, and they don't. I've been on to the station to ask them to find out if he ordered out a taxi from one of the firms. The chauffeur has said he didn't drive him anywhere.'

'Have you been able to discover if anything's missing in the way of clothes?'

'Not yet. I was just about to go inside and have a quick look round.'

'Then we'll go together.'

The kitchen was tidy, with bare table and clean plates and cutlery dry in the plastic rack on the draining-board. The day's *Daily Express* was lying on the floor, where it had fallen after being pushed through the letter flap in the door.

They went upstairs and into the only occupied bedroom. There were few clothes in the old cupboard and few in the chest-of-drawers, but in so far as it was possible to judge, it looked as if at no time had there been many more. Crane looked round the room. There were no photographs or knick-knacks about – but Miles had struck him as a man who had learned to do without such things.

In the bathroom, they found tooth-brush, tooth-paste,

shaving cream, shaving brush, flannel, hair brush, and a large comb.

'Doesn't look very much as if he's cut-and-run for good,' said Retson.

'Unless he had the imagination to set the scene to make it seem he hadn't.' Crane sighed: was there ever a time when one couldn't look on a piece of evidence from at least two directions? 'Let's have a closer look for cheque book and passport.'

Retson found a passport in the breast pocket of the well worn suit, but they came across neither cheque book nor any other indication of easily realizable savings.

The evidence remained inconclusive, thought Crane. If Miles hadn't run, where the hell was he? If he had run . . . Yet he didn't seem the kind of man to run, anymore than he seemed the kind of man to set light to an occupied house . . .

There was a loud call from below which Retson answered. After heralding his appearance with clumping footsteps, a P.C. came into the bedroom. 'There's a message for you from H.Q., sir, just through on the blower.' The constable took out his notebook and opened it. 'The results of tests on the candle wick and wood confirm the similarity between crime and test exhibits numbers one, two, three, and four. Test exhibits five to thirty-four are dissimilar.'

That meant the candle which had been used as a time fuse was exactly similar to the four candles found in this house. They were also similar to candles stocked by the local village store. They were dissimilar to candles bought at every other local store in a radius of six miles and at stores in Ardscastle. Crane ran his fingers through his hair. It was confirmatory evidence, though whether there was even now sufficient proof for Miles to be arrested on a charge of murder and arson he was uncertain. Still, that wasn't his pigeon. The papers would, after Miles had been found and had been questioned once more under caution, be sent to the director of public prosecutions who would advise whether Miles should be charged . . . If only he found it easier to believe in Miles's guilt. . . .

17

'It's nearly five o'clock,' said Anne. 'Would you like some coffee?'

'You're very well domesticated,' he teased. 'Happy?'

'Shall I tell you something, Harry? I'm so happy, I'm worried.'

'That's the worst cack-handed Irishism I've ever heard.' He kissed her.

'Come on, talk to me while I put the coffee on. D'you want something to eat?' She led the way into the kitchen. 'There's not much of a choice for sandwiches: you can have cheese, or go without. We'd better do some shopping before the shops shut. I know some of the things you like, but not everything. What about tomatoes?'

'Only if they're grown on good cow muck to give them flavour.'

'Have I ever told you I don't like cow muck?' She put water and two spoonfuls of ground coffee into the espresso machine.

'You haven't, but I guessed it from the way you tiptoed around the farm.'

She looked across at him. 'Are you returning to the priory?'

'In words of many syllables, no.'

She laughed. 'That'll set them all about their ears.'

'With any luck, it'll give old Smarmy Simon blood pressure.'

There was a ring at the front door. 'Who on earth . . .' she began.

'Electricity,' came the call.

'Norman said there was something wrong with the circuit – have you noticed how the lights sometimes flicker? . . . Put the machine on the stove, will you, while I go and see what they want.'

He screwed on the top of the machine and then lit one of the rings. He heard her open the door.

' 'Morning, lady,' a cheerful voice said. 'Sorry to disturb you, but it won't take long. That right you've got some faulty wiring?'

'There is something wrong. The lights sometime flicker.'

'Can't have that. We'll come in then, shall we? . . . Nice little flat you've got, lady. . . . Shut the door, Alf, or the draught'll freeze the lady. Nice and sunny, but the wind's cold, isn't it?'

Miles sat down. What were Anne and he going to do? He'd have to find a job, of course, because it was impossible to return to the priory. . . .

He heard a dull thump, like a wet towel hitting a wall, and did not bother to try to analyse it.

'Gently, Tom. Nice and cool.'

It was the same speaker he'd heard before, he thought vaguely, but now the other man's name appeared suddenly to be Tom, not Alf. . . . That dull thump. . . . If the queer landlord *had* given away Anne's identity, he could also have given away the fact the electricity was faulty. . . .

He looked round the kitchen. There was a carving knife by the side of the sink, but next to it was a vinegar bottle. He'd learned from bar brawls that a broken bottle was the most dangerous weapon of all in close fighting. He stood up, reached across to the bottle, and crossed to the doorway.

Leading off the far side of the sitting-room was a short passage which gave access to the bedroom and bathroom. One man was standing in the passage entrance and he had hold of Anne under her arm-pits. She was not quite unconscious, but was too dazed to have any control over her limbs. The second man held a hypodermic syringe in his left hand and was filling it from a capsule. They heard him and looked up.

He swung the bottle against the door jamb. He was lucky. It shattered at the mid-way point, leaving him with a saw-toothed half.

The first man, face tightening viciously, dropped Anne to the floor. He swept his hand down to his waist and brought up a flick-knife and he pressed the catch to release the blade. The second man, Alf or Tom, threw the syringe on to the floor and produced a commando style dagger.

Miles came forward at a rush as they began to separate. He thrust the bottle up at the first man's eyes, but the other ducked and lunged forward with the knife, to miss in turn. Alf, choosing his time perfectly and catching Miles slightly off balance, jumped forward. . . . And crashed into Anne, to fall. Miles flicked his wrist round and the jagged glass scored Alf's face, parting the flesh like an over-ripe tomato, only just missing the left eye.

The first man aimed another blow and Miles saw it coming, but just couldn't move quickly enough. The knife sliced his coat and shirt and cut into his right arm, near the elbow. The man came forward and Miles slammed his knee up to catch the other in the crutch. As the man began to double up, Miles slashed the bottle across his face and the lower lip was suddenly hanging down in a flap. There was a burbling scream.

Miles's arm was numbing fast and there was little strength now left in it. Alf, face streaming blood, thrust forward to force Miles to draw back, flicked the dagger to his left hand and feinted a stab. Miles swayed to escape the blow and the dagger was flicked back and then thrust forward.

Miles desperately tried to duck the blow, but was too late : as if everything was suddenly flung into slow motion, he could judge that there was no way in which he could escape and a part of his mind tried to prepare for the white hot agony. Then, when the dagger was almost to his stomach, Alf fell. Miles saw that Anne had grabbed hold of Alf's right ankle. He jammed the bottle down in a corkscrewing motion and Alf clawed frenziedly at his face which was now spurting blood.

The first man was trying to regain his feet. Miles kicked him at the point of his torn mouth and he collapsed, moaning.

There must be others, waiting to come up and carry her off in some form of container. Miles reached down and dragged her to her feet.

She made no move. She was still dazed from the blow and she was shocked by the terrible injuries the men had suffered. A rising tide of nausea made her swallow repeatedly.

Holding on to her with his left hand and the bloody bottle with his right, he dragged her across to the front door. 'Is there a back entrance to the building?' he demanded.

'You ... You turn left at the bottom instead of right.'

He made her race down the two flights of uncovered concrete stairs and he wondered if their clattering footsteps could hope to go unheard. The small entrance hall ended in a passage and that soon turned a right angle so that it was impossible to see far down it. He led the way from the stairs to the passage and when they passed round the right angle he stopped, so unexpectedly she bumped heavily into him. 'Listen,' he whispered. For thirty seconds they heard nothing but the jumble of noises from the street, then there came the clump of footsteps from the entrance hall. He felt her tense, preparing to run with panicky frenzy, and he gripped her hand. 'Wait until they've started upstairs.'

When he reckoned they must be level with the first floor, he said: 'Run like you were doing the mile in three minutes flat.'

They ran, sending a clatter echoing behind them. The passage was another twenty feet long and then there was an unpainted wooden door with a key in the lock. He tried to turn the key with his right hand and found he'd not sufficient strength in it. He used his left hand, but when unlocked the door refused to budge. Christ! he thought, they were caught. ... He forced his mind to control its galloping fears. The light was poor, but he could just make out that the door was bolted top and bottom.

There was a burst of noise, dimly heard along the passage.

Both bolts were stiff and gave only reluctantly. They heard a man shout to enquire if anyone had gone out and although they couldn't hear the answer, they knew it must lead to their way out of the building being discovered.

He hit the bottom bolt with his clenched fist and freed it the final inch. She was gasping, as if she couldn't drag enough air down into her straining lungs. There was another shout: 'Up that passage.' It reached them all too clearly.

He wrenched the door open and they tumbled out into the rubbish-filled courtyard. They skirted a load of rusting tin cans, stumbled through a huge pile of the soggy and tattered remains of cardboard boxes, and reached the eight-foot wide opening out on to the road.

The road was not long to the right and it ended in a T-junction: the houses on either side were terraced, with tiny front gardens. No more than two other persons were walking the pavements. It would be easy to murder them here and get away with it. He ran on, then had to slow down because she could not keep up with him.

The briefest of checks at the T-junction suggested right, a far busier road, was the safer way to take. Half-way along were shops. They continued, scattering some of the pedestrians so that they were followed by curses. A bus passed them and pulled up at a request stop and he tried to increase their pace to make it, but she was panting heavily and could go no faster. He cannoned into a fat woman, who immediately swore at him. The bus began to draw away from the pavement, but with a final effort, when he dragged her with him, they just made it and they breathlessly scrambled on to the platform.

'Nearly missed us, then,' said the conductor, 'but we ain't the last one for the duration, you know.' Then he saw Miles's blood-soaked sleeve. 'Blimey, mate!'

'I've got to get to a hospital,' said Miles.

'You're telling me. Here, love, take your hubby inside and sit him down quick.'

They went inside and sat down on the left-hand row

146

of fore-and-aft seats. Miles stared back through the large rear window. By the request stop, he saw a swirl of people — this could have been caused by men trying to rush through several other people. Then a lorry moved to block his view.

The conductor came through. 'That'll be two at five, or ten the couple and a bargain at half the price! You can't miss the hospital, but I'll give you a shout when we're coming up to it.'

Miles automatically tried to reach down to his right trouser leg pocket for the money and he winced from the sudden stab of pain.

'Forget the lolly,' said the conductor. 'You have this ride on the company. . . . How'd you come to do yourself an injury? Been fighting with the missus?'

'That's right. And she won.'

The conductor winked at Anne. 'As I always says, that's the kind of thing what makes marriage interesting.'

18

As they left the hospital and walked out of the casualty exit, a taxi drew up to discharge an elderly woman. They climbed into the taxi and Miles said to the driver: 'Euston Station, please.'

He settled back into the seat and closed his eyes: they'd given him some pills, but these hadn't really cut out the throbbing pain.

Anne put an arm round him, to hold him against herself in a gesture that was both seeking and giving loving reassurance.

147

He opened his eyes. 'Stop worrying. It didn't happen.'

'I . . . I keep replaying it all in my mind. I've always known how terrible people can be, but actually to see them . . .' She gripped him even more fiercely. 'That bottle . . . Where are we going?'

'A little village, deep in the wilds of the country, where my cousin has a cottage he only uses in mid-summer. No one can ever find us there. . . . By the way, you'll have to become Mrs. Miles. Once the villagers are married, they become very morally-minded.'

She slipped off the plain gold ring from the third finger of her right hand and put it on her left hand. She suddenly kissed him on the side of his cheek. 'It's the strangest honeymoon I've ever been on.'

　　　　■　　　　•　　　　•　　　　•　　　　•

All right,' said Detective Superintendent Moulton aggressively, 'so just what kind of a report can you make now?'

Silly bastard, thought Crane, as he stifled a yawn and wondered if he'd be allowed any sleep that night. He looked across at the detective chief inspector, whose desk was on the other side of the large room on the first floor of county H.Q. The D.C.I. winked.

Moulton, a stringy, juiceless man, said : 'How's it going to look? The chief suspect disappears into the blue and the investigating officer hasn't the slighest idea where.'

'It was a very difficult situation . . .'

'To which you found the wrong solution. You should have sent the papers to the D.P.P. for an immediate ruling on whether Miles should be arrested.'

'I was waiting on the report from the lab concerning the comparison tests on the candle wicks and candle grease.'

'It's very regrettable, Crane, to discover that one of my D.I.s has been in charge of an important case and has, through inefficiency, lost control of . . .'

The telephone on the D.C.I.'s desk rang. Moulton swung round and glared.

The D.C.I. spoke briefly, then replaced the receiver. 'It was a call for Mr. Crane, sir.'

'Wasn't word left that there was to be no interruption?'

'Yes, sir, but this was put through as a matter of importance. There's been a category two sighting of Miles up in London.'

Category two meant that the eye-witness was pretty certain, yet not prepared to be absolutely certain. Crane leaned forward in his chair and an expression of hard eagerness appeared on his face. 'Under what conditions?'

'The P.C. on foot duty only had a brief glimpse of the man and didn't put a name to the face until he was back at the station and had checked with the latest *Gazettes*. He says the man seemed to be in pain and was carrying one arm in a very constrained fashion. As there's a large hospital close by, the P.C. wonders if the man had been going there.'

'I'd better get back on to them right away and ask for an immediate check.'

'Speak to Inspector Peake . . . Here's the number.' The D.C.I. pushed a sheet of paper across his desk and Crane left his chair to pick up that paper.

Moulton looked sourly annoyed. He couldn't help feeling he'd been upstaged.

.   .   .   .   .   .

'Like I told you, Mac,' said Green, 'the boys weren't expecting no one else in the place.'

149

'Dumb bastards.' Reeves did not find it easy to accept and overcome failure. He could never see failure as anything but an insult to himself. He poured himself out another drink. He was a tall, broad-shouldered, handsome man, always careful of his appearance, and usually quietly mannered. When things were going well, there was a lazy, insouciant charm about him which attracted and hid the cruel arrogance.

Green fiddled with a cigarette. He wasn't afraid of Reeves, but did feel slightly uneasy in the face of such single-minded viciousnesss.

Reeves crossed to a chair and sat down. 'We've got to get her. Until she's cold, we're at risk . . . See Oliver and find out everything he knows about the broad.'

'But we've . . .' Green stopped.

Reeves looked up, with slightly narrowed eyes. 'So we've talked to him. Talk again and this time find out something fresh. . . . Have you got the flat staked out?'

Green nodded. He was convinced that the men who were watching the flat where Mary Walsh had been living were wasting their time – she was too smart to return. But Reeves gave the orders.

'Get moving, then.'

Green obediently left the flat.

Reeves drained the glass. A fortune at risk, he thought, and largely because of one broad. Until she was dead – along with the mug of a cowman she was with . . .

He lit a cigarette. He had long, elegant fingers and he took great care to keep them well manicured. One of the things which most disgusted him about prison was the way his hands became work-worn and dirt-ingrained.

He remembered the first time he'd met the new prison visitor – Pattison. He hated all prison visitors because he was convinced that their only reason for visiting was the holier-than-thou uplift they gained from their work.

He'd sized up Pattison with expert ease. He could identify a man who was ever on the make. And he'd laughed to himself over the months as he'd watched and listened and Pattison had approached closer and closer to what was uppermost in his mind, but had never quite dared to come out with it. In the end, he'd forced Pattison's hand by bluntly asking what that move was.

The move had been good, but crude – until he'd refined it by utilizing his expert knowledge of police routine. It had been his idea to initiate the fake attack on the broad, the theft of the candles and the lapel badge (this, of course, by lucky chance), the wearing of a ring inscribed with a loving message from a fictitious husband . . .

When he thought of Mary Walsh, he longed to have her in front of him, a chiv in his hand . . .

Her disappearance days before the mark could have thrown anyone, but it hadn't thrown him. He'd seen a way through and had sent word to Baird to find a woman who'd near enough resemble Mary Walsh if she were well and truly burned. What had the woman's name been? He couldn't remember. But she'd been so dumb she'd believed everything she'd been told and had gone towards her death thinking only of the grand she'd been promised. Still, Pattison had gone towards his death thinking only of the fortune he was making . . .

Everything had moved smoothly. After the fire, they'd even quickly managed to pick up Mary Walsh's trail through the landlord of the queer's pub. But then the two who'd gone to take her had met a man with a broken bottle. . . .

He swore, crudely and repetitiously.

. . . . . .

For a couple of years, Oliver Baird had begun to fatten: his cheeks were noticeably plump and a double chin was in the offing. There was now a hint of slack debauchery about his sleek looks and nothing he could do – since he had not the strength of character to rearrange his life – would hide the fact.

Green said: 'Try thinking.'

'I've told you, Sam. I could murder my brain and there still wouldn't be anything fresh.' Baird sat behind a large desk in a room on the first floor above the drinking club he ran.

Green despised Baird. Baird was a fixer, often useful even necessary, yet too soft to do a big job himself. 'I need to find her,' said Green flatly.

'I told you all I know, last time. So why don't you . . .'

'Keep the questions,' snapped Green.

Baird hurriedly began to repeat all he knew about Mary Walsh and Green listened and tried to pick up one new fact which would give him a lead.

Baird finally stopped talking, ran a pink tongue along over-red lips, and fidgeted. Green had learned nothing fresh. Yet he hesitated to return to Reeves and report no dice. 'She must've known someone else than what you've mentioned: someone she'd ask for help?'

'If she did, I never heard the name.'

Green had an idea, not directly introduced by anything Baird had said. 'What's she going to use for spending money? The mug she's with hasn't any. D'you think she'll get back to acting? Who was her agent?'

Baird shrugged his shoulders.

'You're making out you don't know bloody nothing.'

Baird looked scared.

'What did she do with her money?'

'I don't know, straight.'

'Was she a big spender?'

'Her? She spent like it hurt.'

'Then maybe she was saving for her old age.' Green's voice quickened. 'And maybe she's going to have to start using some of it now.'

'Could be. But if you try to ask me where she put it . . .'

'Ask you, you stupid bastard? She left the flat real quick and her handbag's around. There's maybe a cheque book in it that'll tell us.' How had he overlooked such an obvious lead until now?

. . . . .

Crane, back from county H.Q. and in his own office, had his tie off and his shirt undone at the neck. He'd drunk four cups of coffee in the past half hour as he'd waited for the call and was so tired that there was a band of pain behind his eyes.

He lit another cigarette and was half-way through it when the phone finally rang. He grabbed the receiver. 'Detective Inspector speaking.'

'P.C. three nought one, sir. Mr. Peake told me to ring you.'

Crane listened to the report. The man had had a bad cut on his right arm, needing considerable stitching. He'd given the hospital his name, address, and other normal details, and all these had been checked out and found to be false. The duty out-patients' doctor had queried the cause of the cut and the patient had said his wife had been holding a carving knife to show him a nick on the blade and he had stumbled on to it: his wife had confirmed this story. The doctor had been doubtful, but not doubtful enough to make any sort of an issue of it.

'Did you say his wife?' asked Crane.

'That's right, sir. She was with him at the hospital.'

Crane thought about that. There'd never been the slightest suggestion that Miles had a living wife. So had he teamed up with a woman since fleeing the priory? But that made it really quick work. Miles's grief at Anne O'Reilly's death had been genuine and a man of his character surely didn't switch from being tragically desolated to living with another woman in a matter of days? . . . Remembering how Miles had refused to believe the news of Anne O'Reilly's pregnancy . . . that the taxi driver who had driven Anne O'Reilly out to the priory that last night had said her face was largely obscured and she spoke very little. 'Did you see his wife?'

'She was helping him along, but like my attention was caught by him, I didn't take any notice of her.'

'Just detail what you do remember.'

There was a pause. 'She wasn't tall, just medium height, and she wasn't young and dolly pretty. More kind of homely and warm, if you know what I mean. She'd black hair, very curly . . . That's all, I'm afraid, sir.'

'It's enough. Make out a G forty-three, will you, and send it down. And tell Mr. Peake I'm very grateful for all your help.'

Crane replaced the receiver. The description was very poor, yet he was certain the woman was Anne O'Reilly. . . . The case was exploding. This morning had begun with one or two queries, the night was ending with so many there wasn't room for them all to stand up and be counted. If Anne O'Reilly was alive, who had died in the fire? Why? Who'd made the substitution? – Miles had certainly believed her dead, so he hadn't . . .

Everything stemmed from the fire. Either Miles had set the fire, in league with Anne O'Reilly – but this possibility had surely become unlikely? – or she had been mixed up in some sort of villainy to which Miles had not been a party and she or a third person had set the fire. . . . Had this first gone wrong when she fell in love with Miles? . . .

He tried to pin down his whirling thoughts. Hadn't someone told him that Anne O'Reilly had sharply given one of the young tractor drivers the cold shoulder, yet had made friends almost on sight with Miles? Something more than natural attraction? What about the attack on her? Miles had seemingly managed to save her in the nick of time? Faked? Part of the plan? What plan? . . . The paintings were worth a million quid, plus. But experts had testified that the remains seemed authentic . . . Remains could be faked: clever forgers were always making fools of art experts. The Spaniard had been working in the house: had he been faking, not cleaning? Was his death no accident? Had Anne O'Reilly read the news of his death in Madrid and taken fright? Had another woman been substituted in her place, to head off any deep investigation into her? . . . Pattison must have been in on the original swindle. Why not? The line dividing keen business from smart villainy was often thin. Then he'd been murdered, almost skilfully enough to make his death seem accidental . . . And because there was a further crime to which Pattison had not been a party . . .

Crane stood up, crossed to the nearer filing cabinet, slid open the top drawer, and brought out a green folder. He returned to his desk and opened the folder. The dead woman in the priory had been five foot seven, aged between thirty-five and forty-five, weight around eleven stone, hair black and curly, two months' pregnant, in good physical shape. He wrote out those few physical details. The lists of missing persons must be checked.

•   •   •   •   •

Reeves, looking as fresh and as wide awake as if it were the middle of the morning and not the night, said: 'So?'

'So I went to the flat and checked her handbag,' said Green. 'There was a bank book in it.'

Reeves merely nodded.

Green knew a quick flash of annoyance: it had been a smart bit of thinking and it wouldn't have choked Reeves to say so. 'She's got a deposit account with the National Westminster in Gumton Street.'

'How much?'

'More'n three grand.'

Reeves silently whistled. 'So now all we need is someone in that bank who's tender. Find him.'

Green stood up. It was always easy to give orders.

'And Sam,' said Reeves. 'Oliver knows we're hot about Mary. So when she croaks, he'd not need to read the papers to know who. Along with him not seeing that other broad again, he'd have too much news.'

Green nodded.

'Make it seem natural.'

19

The cottage was at the end of a blind lane which had grass and nettle covered four foot high earth banks. The garden was small and unkempt and fields beyond sloped away to give distant views of Rushington.

Their nearest general store was half a mile away, in the village of Ensham, and on the morning following their arrival Miles took Anne along and introduced her as his wife. They were congratulated on their marriage in ribald

156

terms which made her wonder how accurate had been his previous description of the local inhabitants. The owner of the store happily agreed to their having a weekly account and they bought a quantity of food.

Back in the cottage, with a fire in the sitting-room for the sake of cheerfulness rather than warmth, Anne made him lie down on the settee. He fell asleep and when he awoke it was twelve o'clock.

'I let you sleep on, Harry, because it's the best possible thing for you. Will you have something to eat or drink now, or wait until lunch?'

He yawned. 'I could surely go a cup of strong coffee.' Without thought, he moved his right arm and the sharp pain made him tighten his mouth.

'I'll get you one of those pills the hospital gave you. They said you can take one every four hours.'

She kissed him and left, soon returning with a pill and a glass of water.

'I'll go and make the coffee,' she said, after he'd swallowed the pill. She hesitated, then spoke with a rush and her expression suggested she'd tried to keep silent, but couldn't. 'Harry – what are we going to do?'

He looked directly at her. She'd the courage of two, he thought, but even so she'd been taken right to the limits of her self-control. He patted the settee and she came and sat down by him. 'I'll tell you. Just as soon as my arm's fit enough, we'll have fun.'

She smiled briefly. 'I seem to have found a man with a one-track mind.'

'Two tracks merely confuse direction.'

'Be serious, darling, just for a moment. What are we going to do now?' Her voice sharpened.

He took hold of her right hand. 'We're going to do nothing.'

'But . . .'

'Tucked away here, an army couldn't find us. We're safer than we could be anywhere else. There's only one problem – money.'

'That's no problem,' she said immediately. 'I . . .' She cleared her throat. 'I always promised myself that one day I'd escape the kind of life I was in. Even when I got in deeper than ever. I can't explain it . . .'

'Don't try,' he said softly.

'You must know everything. Don't you see, it's only if you do that I can feel that . . . that there's nothing left which can unexpectedly turn up and shock you so much it breaks us up.'

He raised her hand and kissed it.

'The money I saved was my lifeline to a decent life, even though the money was itself rotten. I . . . I even put what Pattison and you gave me into the bank . . .'

He laughed. It was clearly not the reaction she had expected. 'Don't you see, Anne, the delightful irony of it? We're going to enjoy life on the money Pattison paid out to further some sort of swindle. We'll buy champagne and drink to the old bastard and if I'm any judge of character that'll hurt him more than the bed of red-hot coals he's resting on.'

She looked uncertain, even shocked.

'How much cash have you got?' he asked.

'Quite . . . quite a lot,' she answered, not naming a sum.

'Enough to keep us going until the summer?'

'More than that.'

'Then the present is wonderful and nothing else exists. Go down to the local store and ask 'em to pick up a case of champagne from town: the old boy'll always bring stuff back for his customers. There's nothing heals an injured arm as quickly as champagne.'

'I think I really ought to keep you on a diet of water.'

•   •   •   •   •

Baird made an untidy corpse. He had fallen head first from his office and although the drop was only thirteen feet from the window-ledge, his head had taken the initial impact. His body, curling round to the right, looked quite obese, much more so than when he'd been alive.

The police surgeon was a man with a peculiar sense of humour. 'Well, I can tell you one thing for sure. He's dead.'

The uniform sergeant did not smile. He wondered how long it would be before some lazy bastard from C.I.D. stirred himself sufficiently to come along and take over. Not that there was so far any suggestion of criminal death: but since Baird had a record, it was a C.I.D. matter.

'You said there's a three parts empty bottle of whisky up top?' asked the police surgeon. 'As I've always held, that's the way to go. Too tight to care. I'll give you ten to one the P.M. finds the blood alcohol level was nearer point four than point two.'

The sergeant was not a betting man.

•   •   •   •   •

To an untrained observer, a man could usually disguise himself sufficiently to be unrecognizable at a later date. Green had plumped out his cheeks with pads, added a small, well trimmed moustache, tinted his hair ginger with a wash and parted it almost at the centre. He wore shoes a full size too small so that he had a noticeably strange walk. His clothes were ill-fitting and shabby. A policeman would be able to see through the points of disguise and so identify him, but Mrs. Thomas would never do so.

'I ... I don't know,' she said helplessly.

'Look, lady, you've got to know.'

She brushed a stray hair from her forehead.

'You're in the books for two hundred and fifty-three.'

'I really don't see how it can be that much. I know I ...'

'What's your old man going to say? What's the bank going to say?'

She looked as if she was going to break into tears. Green's expression became still more contemptuous.

'Surely they'll give me more credit?' she asked.

'Lady, for you credit's a word that's gone out of use.' If he'd talked about gambling debts due to anyone of intelligence, that person would have known the needle was being pointed.

'They've always given me credit in the past,' she persisted.

Had she once been young and attractive? And what had first hooked her on horse racing? 'Lady, I need that two hundred and fifty-three. Today. Now.'

She carefully stirred her cup of tea. The café was small, rather grimy, with bare wooden tables and the menu written on a slate, but the tea was good. She sipped the tea, replaced the cup on the chipped saucer. 'I suppose I could give you two pounds fifty now and ...'

He sighed. 'Lady, don't we communicate at all? I want the whole gazoop. That way, everyone stays healthy.'

She wasn't stupid and she had understood at least part of the threat, but until now she'd vainly hoped that if she ignored it, it would melt away. She decided to appeal to his better nature. 'My husband doesn't earn much at the bakery and although we keep trying to save, Joan — that's our girl — she's got trouble with that husband of hers . . .'

'You'll have me crying . . . Two hundred and fifty-three quid.'

'I . . . I can't possible give you that much money.'

'Then that's tough on you. And tough on your little girl with all the husband trouble.'

'How d'you mean?'

'Lady, I just give messages. But I know the boys and if they don't get paid, they get nasty.'

'How can I?' she asked, in little more than a whisper.

'How can't you, lady, knowing your little girl might get striped with a chiv?'

She stared at him with shocked disbelief. 'No one would do such a terrible thing.'

Didn't she ever watch the telly? he wondered.

'I haven't got two hundred and fifty-three pounds. I told you . . .'

'Then it's going to get tough for you. Unless . . .'

She grabbed at the chance he seemed to offer her 'Unless what?'

'Maybe if you gave the boys a little information I know they want . . . They're not unreasonable. You do them a favour, likely they do you one.'

'What information?'

'Like when and where a certain client starts drawing out money.'

She stared at him with fresh disbelief: nightmare was piling up on top of nightmare. 'I couldn't do anything like that. In a bank there has to be complete client security.'

'Lady, you're mediaeval. You ain't no options. You talk and no one knows nothing, you don't talk and your hubby and the bank learns you've been gambling something crazy and your little girl wakes up to find she's got a different face.'

She was a woman with a degree of courage and determination which came from stubborn adherence to certain principles in life and she might have faced the threats to herself, accepting them as just retribution for her own weak stupidity, but she was quite unequipped to defy the threat of physical violence to her only daughter.

. . . . .

Crane handled a telephone call concerning a break-in in a farmhouse, then pulled across the desk the typed note Oliveland had dropped in as he'd started the call.

Eight women on the missing persons lists were possibles for the dead woman in the priory. All were within the limits of height, size, age, and all had black curly hair.

He re-read the names, becoming selective. Five women could reasonably be dismissed because they had been missing for months. Of the remaining three, one woman was believed on strong evidence to be in France. The two remaining women must be checked right out. Since both had last lived in London, it was London's job.

He phoned the county liaison officer at New Scotland Yard and asked the other to put through the two requests to the divisions or departments concerned. When he replaced the receiver, he sighed. The case was tantalizingly short of hard facts and as a result Mouldy Moulton was forever moaning, the press was being a nuisance, and the insurance assessor and investigator were making his life a burden with their incessant demands to say, once and for all, whether the paintings had been destroyed by fire or had been stolen and that only worthless copies had been burned. . . .

    •   •   •   •   •

In direct contradiction to the forecast, the weather became warm and sunny. Hardly a breath of wind stirred the fresh green leaves of the trees or rippled the, now, fast growing grass.

They sat out in the garden, in two deck-chairs which had seen much better days.

'Harry,' said Anne suddenly, 'I can't forget . . .'

'You can, since there's no past,' he interrupted.

She fiddled with a frayed edge of the canvas seat. 'Sometimes, it's not that easy.'

'Work harder at forgetting whatever it is you've got to forget.'

'But then what about the future?'

'Too far away to exist.'

'You're saying we're to bury ourselves in never-never land?'

'Why not?'

'I . . . I don't think it's really possible.'

'But you can't know for certain until you've tried it.'

'When did you discover how to become so completely indolent?'

'Bumming around the Mediterranean.'

'But you told me you worked there from time to time?'

'Only in order to be able to become more indolent.'

She smiled. 'You're quite impossible. You refuse to discuss anything seriously.'

'Quite.'

163

She closed her eyes and let her arms flop down by her sides. 'I was so determined to face serious reality. But you've completely undermined all my resolutions.'

'Good. That's the second step towards total dissolution.'

'And the first, no doubt, was meeting you? I'm glad I'm being dissolved.'

.   .   .   .   .

Mrs. Thomas left the bank where she worked and walked along Gumton Street. She had had a straightforward, uncomplicated nature until recently, yet now she found she kept asking herself questions to which there were no answers, judging her own actions with contempt, and knowingly twisting the truth into lies because these were easier to live with.

She approached the call box opposite the cinema, moving very hurriedly when she caught sight of a distant blue uniform because she became irrationally afraid the policeman would guess what treason she was committing.

Inside, she went to put some coins on top of the box and met her reflection in the small mirror. She couldn't understand why she didn't look any different.

She dialled the number she had been given and held a twopence piece ready. Pray God, she thought, that there was no answer. Her prayer went unheard. She inserted the coin with fingers which suddenly trembled. 'It's … it's me.'

'Well?'

'I've managed to get what you want. I told the head cashier …'

'Forget the details. What's the address?'

'It's the main branch in Wottom Street in Rushington.

Miss Walsh has so far cashed one hundred and ten pounds.'

'What's the broad's address?'

'I don't know that. You see, all we were told . . .'

The connexion was cut.

She replaced the receiver. She moved to her right and once more stared at the reflection of her lined, tired, hard-worked face. Twenty years of honest, faithful work, be-trayed in seconds. The mark of Judas was on her.

The burden of her own iniquity was so pressing that she knew, with sudden and violent certainty, she couldn't bear it unaided. She had to tell someone what had hap-pened, because then something could be done to lessen the degree of her treachery. If she informed the police, without identifying herself, they'd find out what was hap-pening. . . .

With desperate eagerness, she dialled 999. She asked for the police and told the man she spoke to that she worked in a bank and had just been forced to divulge confidential information, to wit, that a Miss Mary Walsh was drawing money from her account in Rushing-ton. No, she replied, she certainly would not give her own name, nor would she say where she was speaking from, nor would she describe by what means she'd been forced to give the man the information.

When she left the telephone kiosk, she felt better.

.   .   .   .   .   .

The duty inspector picked out the form which had reached him in the endless slotted belt and he read the report. An unidentified woman had been forced in an undisclosed manner to tell an unidentified man that Miss Mary Walsh was drawing money from her account in

Rushington. Hell! thought the duty inspector sardonically, police work would be a lot easier if only it weren't for the public.

20

Reeves crossed to the window and looked down at the window-box in which large pansies were forming a splash of colour. 'How many know her on sight?'

Green, hair and face normal, smartly dressed, no longer the traveller in vulgar novelties, said: 'Only Figs and Alec what did the job with her in the country. But there must be several people what saw her when she was with Oliver...'

'We don't bring anyone fresh in.' Reeves returned from the window and crossed to the fireplace: he faced the room, resting his elbows on the mantelpiece. 'Send the two to watch the bank. When she turns up, they find out where she's living with the cowman.'

'We can't make it look like an accident, Mac, and have it stick.'

'Yeah?' Reeves spoke with contemptuous sarcasm. 'Then maybe I'd better think again.'

Green cursed himself for being so stupid as to believe Reeves had not a plan completely formulated.

•   •   •   •   •

Crane was just leaving his car, having parked it in the courtyard, when Oliveland came across.

'We've word in on Grace Brent and Linda Elliott,' said Oliveland.

Crane struggled to remember who they were, certain the detective sergeant was getting a perverse amusement from testing his memory. He finally did remember. 'Well? Do I get the report today? Is there any clear tie-up with the priory?'

Oliveland looked vaguely annoyed that Crane had managed to identify the names. 'There's no tie-up that I can see.' He brought a sheet of paper from his pocket.

Crane leaned against his car as he read the details. Two women, approaching middle age, one married, one single, suddenly and recently vanished. Mrs. Grace Brent had been a housewife, ordinary in every respect except she'd suffered from severe depression : Miss Linda Elliott had inhabited the twilight world where honesty merged into dishonesty, virtue into vice, love into prostitution. He read the last sentence concerning Linda Elliott and looked up. 'It says she was friendly with Oliver Baird. Don't we know that name?'

Oliveland thought, but it was clear the name meant nothing to him.

Crane said : 'I'm sure it rings a bell, but what that bell sounds like. . . . He was in the news recently, that's for sure.'

Oliveland scratched his right ear.

'Shuffle through the bumf and see if you can put some facts to the name.'

'I've a hell of a lot of work . . .' began Oliveland.

'And now you've a little more. Don't despair. One day they'll put up the pay of overworked detective sergeants.'

Oliveland, looked disgruntled, left. Crane went up to his room, sat, stared at the paperwork, and sighed. An army marched on its stomach : a police force crawled on its paperwork.

He was signing the last of the three detective constables' notebooks when Oliveland entered the room.

Oliveland spoke abruptly. 'Oliver Baird was a villains' pimp and banker.'

'Was?'

'He very recently fell out of the window of his office and discovered concrete's harder than human bone.'

Crane had suffered enough for one day of Oliveland's irritating manner. 'Would it be too much trouble to make a proper report?'

Oliveland looked contentedly aggrieved and spoke in a very flat, official voice. 'He fell from his office on the first floor, landed on his head, and was killed instantly. The P.M. discovered he'd been drinking heavily and the inquest found he died an accidental death. Sir.'

Accidental? There was nothing to say it wasn't, except the very tenuous theory that Linda Elliott had been the woman who'd died in the priory fire. Yet the mob – accepting the even more tenuous theory there was one – behind the priory murders had, in the first instance, tried to make those murders look like accidents and villains often kept using the same successful method. . . . Crane looked up. 'Get back on to the county laision officer and ask him for full information on Baird, with special reference to all known female contacts. Send him up as complete a description of Anne O'Reilly as we have and ask him to follow through Linda Elliot's history.'

•   •   •   •   •

Figs Allport, so nicknamed because of his passion for dried figs, was not clever in the conventional sense, yet he was possessed of a high degree of cunning common-sense and he had the patience of two Jobs. Even after an hour's watch from a car, he was still so alert that he identified Mary Walsh immediately. He saw her walk along the pavement, from the direction of the traffic lights, and enter the bank.

When she emerged, she began to walk back towards the traffic lights. He started the engine and depressed the clutch to engage first gear and at that moment a delivery van double-parked to cut him off. About to tell the van driver to get lost, he checked the angry words and switched off the engine. At all costs, he must not draw attention to himself. Now they knew for certain their information had been correct, they could set up a more elaborate trap for her next visit.

.   .   .   .   .

There were two days of overcast skies, drizzle, and gusting winds which kept threatening to turn into gales but never quite made it. Then the winds departed, the clouds thinned, and there was scattered sunshine.

At four-fifteen on the afternoon of the third day, a message from the county liaison officer came through on the Telex (preceded by a code figure to remind county they were paying full transmission charges).

The message was very concisely worded, yet was still long because the ramifications of Baird's work had been considerable. The attached list of women acquaintances contained twenty-one names and against one of these, Mary Walsh, was a note that her name had been mentioned in an unusual 999 call: a précis of that call was given.

It was like a jig-saw puzzle, thought Crane, in which every piece was of the same design so that it was only when one saw a complete and coherent picture, or a visual jumble, that one knew whether the pieces were in the right places. Mary Walsh, present whereabouts not known, had been a friend of Baird who had apparently died an accidental death. Baird had known Linda Elliot, whose present whereabouts was not known. Linda Elliott had been roughly the same shape, size, and age, as the supposedly dead Anne O'Reilly. Did these facts interlock to form a lucid picture, or did they interlock merely to complete a meaningless jumble?

Oliveland would have plumped for the meaningless jumble, because it needed a conscious effort of imagination to believe otherwise. Crane, however, decided to act on them. He rang the Rushington police.

21

It was just dark and the night air had a balmy quality which suggested fine, warm weather ahead. In the sitting-room of the cottage, the ancient black and white television set was showing the first episode of a new series. This had only been on for a few minutes when Miles said : 'Do we really want to watch this?'

'You tell me,' replied Anne. 'Do we?'

'No.' He switched off the set, then returned to sit close by her.

'Now tell me something, Harry. What was so wrong with the programme that "we" didn't like it?'

'It's that the whole set-up was so bogus. At a guess, the writer and director had either never been to the south of Spain or else had visited it for no more than a day.'

170

'How was it bogus?'

'In its atmosphere. The coast is hot and sunny, of course – in summer – but only a tiny handful of super-rich lead the kind of life the so-called hero was supposedly living. There aren't a multitude of servants any longer, because they've become too expensive. You don't eat imported food, especially cheese, and you don't drink French wine, because anything imported costs very much more than the local product.'

'All right, so that's just bringing old-style Hollywood to the idiots' box. But were they correct to suggest it's a different world, cut off from reality?'

'Well I suppose there's more truth in that than the rest of their miserable effort. Down there, in the sun, living under the rule of mañana, the outside world does seem a long, long way away. I always remember when the U.K. was having one of its perennial labour crises and there was the threat of anarchic strikes and the local paper in English headlined the shattering news that the millionth visitor had just flown in to the nearest airport and had been greeted with a glass of champagne. The crisis in the U.K. was relegated to a small paragraph on page five.'

'It sounds ideal.'

Her tone of voice made him look quickly at her. 'It's wonderful for a time, but very lotus-eating after that.'

'You're always telling me there isn't a day after today . . . Harry, will you take me to the sleepiest, most away-from-it-all place you know?'

'What's the trouble? Has our own never-never land come to a stop?'

She nibbled her lip. 'I . . . I'm being stupid.'

'That's surely every woman's prerogative?'

'I know it's only my imagination, but . . .'

'But what?'

She seemed to draw a deep breath. 'But when I left the bank this morning, I think I was followed.'

Because this was the last thing he had expected, his response was automatic. 'It's impossible. You were imagining it.'

'I suppose so. I . . . I told you I was being silly.'

He reminded himself she had shown herself to be a woman who was anything but silly. 'Tell me exactly what happened?'

Her forehead puckered and she clasped her fingers together round her right knee. 'I went to the bank to cash a cheque and when I came out I started to walk towards the lights. Then I suddenly remembered I'd got to go to the bakers to buy a loaf and I abruptly stopped and turned. There was a man about twenty yards away who was looking directly at me and there was a momentary expression of consternation on his face, as if I'd caught him out.'

He deliberately spoke lightly. 'He'd been leching after you and was scared you'd shout for the police and have him arrested for obscene thoughts.'

She shook her head. 'He was years younger than me and certainly not interested in mutton when there was so much lamb about . . . But that's not the end of things. I walked past him and went into the bakers and bought a brown wholemeal loaf, came out, and started up the road again. The feeling I was being followed became so strong that I went into a chemist, there acted as if I'd forgotten something and came straight out. The same man was next door, apparently staring into a shoe shop.'

'And did he take any notice of you?'

'He was very careful not to.'

'But that's just your interpretation of a non-event. Anne, it simply has to be a coincidence. If for no other reason, then because it's impossible anyone could begin to know we're within a hundred miles of here.'

She spoke with stubborn defensiveness. 'Why was he so interested in me?'

'He wasn't, but you thought he was.'

'I didn't imagine the look on his face.'

'All right. But you could easily have misunderstood it. He happened to be looking in your direction, you turned round suddenly, and he found you looked like his favourite aunt...'

'He wasn't the kind of person to have a favourite aunt.'

'In what way, wasn't he?'

'He looked meanly vicious. I know the type – he was some kind of villain.'

The past tensions had finally caught her out, he thought. He remembered, still with shame, although there was nothing to be ashamed about, the day on leave when a flying bomb had exploded quite a way away from where he'd been walking. People had stared with sneering wonder at him because he'd all but collapsed as the delayed horror of the sinking of the T.S.S. *Oakmore*, a horror until then suppressed, had surfaced to overwhelm him. He told her how he'd trembled from head to foot that afternoon.

'So all I've got to do,' she began, 'is to pull myself together...'

'On the contrary. Let yourself go completely. Get it all out of your system. And then you'll be in fine form to go to Puerto de Tendraitx.'

'When I think what life would be like without you ... Tell me about this place.'

'It's a little harbour, on the one stretch of the Mediterranean coast the tourists haven't discovered and ruined. Nothing ever happens in Spain, but in Puerto de Tendraitx nothing happens twice as often. There's one tiny hotel where the wife cooks like a genius, the locals are charming and endlessly courteous and as far as they're concerned Madrid is so far away it may not really exist.'

'Sun, sea, solitude. How soon can we go?'

'As soon as we've got over the snag of passports. Mine's back at Priory Cottage and I daren't return for it.'

'No problem. We'll buy two fresh ones.'

'Buy?' he said.

'When you're in the know, there's nothing you can't buy if you've the money. For three hundred . . .' She stopped because there was a sharp noise from the hall which caught both their attentions and made them mentally query what had caused it.

Before he could go outside to check, the door was swung open. Three men, two armed with pick-axe handles, one with a canvas, sand-filled cosh, pushed inside. Their expressions were similar : a mixture of tension, anticipation, and savage intention.

Miles, knowing any fight must be hopeless, prepared to fight. He rolled off the settee and on to the floor, swung round.

He was too slow. A pick-axe handle slammed into his side, not cleanly, but hard enough to jolt fierce pain through his body. He heard Anne scream, a tortured ringing sound which was cut off in mid pitch. Desperately, he lunged for the small lopsided wooden table on which was an ornamental paper knife : a futile weapon, yet a weapon. A blow across his back knocked him down on all fours.

'What d'you want?' he heard Anne cry. 'If it's money . . .'

'It ain't money.' The speaker laughed coarsely. 'And seeing your age, lady, it ain't the other thing, either.'

174

'Then what are you after?' she persisted wildly.

'You and this mug,' said a second man briskly.

'In God's name, why?'

'Come on, Mary, you ain't soft. You know the score … Here, get that mug moving.'

'One mug moving, Mac.' A shoe thudded into Miles's right side. 'On your feet, lover-boy.'

He made a grab for a leg and managed to get hold of it, but could not summon enough strength to pull the man off balance.

Someone laughed. 'He loves you, Alec, like crazy.'

The foot kicked clear and stamped down on his hand, making him cry out from the pain.

'You're killing him,' said Anne wildly. 'Leave him alone.'

'You tell him to leave us alone. Don't he ever learn, lady?'

Miles heard a smothered curse and then a furious: 'She tried to claw me.'

'Wild! Know something? If she fights that good, maybe she's not too old after all. Let's have a quick feel to see … Here, I'll take these for starters.'

Anne screamed again.

'Chuck it.'

'Mac, all I want…'

'There ain't no secret about what you want. . . . Get that mug moving or we'll be here all night.'

Miles was dragged to his feet. He consciously concentrated all his strength into his right arm and swung. His blow was blocked with ease and his arm was twisted up behind his back in a lock which immediately crippled him. He was forced past Anne and into the hall.

'Steve,' ordered Mac, now out in the hall and standing by the foot of the staircase, 'get on outside and check all's smooth.'

A man pushed past Miles, opened the front door, and went out.

'Where are you taking us?' mumbled Miles, finding his tongue had become clumsy.

He was not answered. 'Anne,' he called out, 'are you all right? Have they hurt you?'

'Not . . . not really,' she answered, in a low voice into which she managed to instill some measure of composure. She realized, with terrifying clarity, that these men had not bothered to conceal their faces because they had no fear that either she or Harry would ever be in a position to testify against them. Now, her one aim was to prevent his guessing the truth until it could no longer be escaped. 'How badly are you hurt?'

He lied, his motives partially the same as hers. 'I'm fine, just a little . . .'

'Shove it,' said Mac roughly. He spoke to Alec. 'What's keeping Steve?'

'He always was a slow moving bastard,' answered Alec.

There was suddenly the screeching cry of a nearby little owl, a sound so unexpected and shrill that they both started. Shamefacedly, they then tried to give the impression that it had not startled them.

'Please . . . please let us go,' said Anne. 'I could give you . . .'

Mac cursed her as he tried to catch the sound of the returning footsteps of Steve. When he failed to hear them, he said : 'Get out, Alec, and kick Steve back in here.'

'What about this mug?'

'Christ!' shouted Mac, suddenly losing his self-control. 'Do I have to hand-feed you. Flick him.'

The words held no definite meaning for Miles, but he tensed himself to fight. The arm lock was released, catching him unawares, then the cosh slammed down on to the back of his neck to crash him into unconsciousness.

He regained consciousness in three stages. First, he had an awareness, though not of anything specific: next he knew a throbbing pain which washed backwards and forwards deep inside his skull: finally he both remembered the past and became aware of the present. Anne was sitting on the stairs, her face twisted with fright, and Mac was moving uneasily, pacing towards the front door and then back again.

They all heard the clump of approaching footsteps. Miles was far too dazed to read any significance into their sound, but Mac reacted immediately. He stared for one brief moment at the hall window, made opaque by darkness, with a disbelief so overwhelming that under other circumstances his expression would have been ludicrously funny, then he turned and ran.

Miles acted without thought: he stuck out his right foot. Mac caught it with the toe of his left shoe, crashed forward, and suffered a damaging blow from the pick-axe handle he still held in his right hand.

The front door opened and into the house first stepped a uniformed P.C., peak cap pushed well back on his head, broad shoulders slightly hunched. Behind him followed Steve and Alec and behind them a second P.C., who had a powerful and heavy torch, switched on, in his right hand.

The first P.C., careful not to lose sight of Mac, said to Steve in a voice of irony: 'And you nearly had us believing you were here all on your own.'

Mac struggled to his feet. The first P.C. didn't give the impression of moving very quickly, yet he had a firm grip on the pick-axe handle by the time Mac regained his feet. He brought the handle down on Mac's head with plenty of vigour. 'Now let's not any of us get too excited, eh?'

22

It was a warm, crisp, sunny day, with the air so clear that the distant views of Rushington were sharply focussed. Crane sat in one of the deck-chairs and Anne in the other : Miles had brought out a kitchen chair.

Miles's tone of voice was harsh. 'So you've got no further?'

Crane ran the palm of his hand over his hair in a weary gesture. He admired the kind of courage which made a man fight on and on and was sadly disappointed that he could not reward such courage with better news.

'You said you reckoned to be able to tie it all up so that Anne would be in the clear...'

'Not completely in the clear. In a position where at the worst Miss Walsh would receive a suspended sentence from the courts.' He remembered too late that they far preferred the name of Anne O'Reilly. 'I'm sorry, but nothing can hide the fact that when she went down to the priory she knew she was being asked to do something illegal.'

'But I didn't know what,' she objected tightly.

Crane sighed. 'The law always wants its pound of flesh. If a person knows she is doing something wrong, even if she's no idea of the degree of wrong, she's held at least in part responsible for the consequences.'

'So Anne theoretically bears some responsibility. But very little by any reasonable standards.' Miles spoke with the anger of fear. They had been so close to disaster and yet survived that it seemed totally wrong Anne should now be in any danger.

Crane offered cigarettes. 'As I said right at the beginning, the real trouble is that we cannot locate the paintings. They prove there was a third layer to the crime. Without the proof that they were stolen and not burned in the fire — and don't forget the burnt scraps were good enough for experts to declare them as consistent with having come from the genuine paintings — and in the face of the complete silence of Reeves and his mob, we cannot prove to a court of law that a third layer ever existed.'

'If there wasn't the third layer, why should Reeves have tried to kill Anne and me?'

'He refuses to give any reason and denies anything beyond assault. We cannot prove the motive until we find the paintings.'

'But the inference has to be . . .'

'Courts don't like inferences.'

'All right, then. What about the fact that Anne ran away from the priory and another woman's body was substituted?'

'It could be said, couldn't it, that Mrs. O'Reilly' — this time he remembered — 'was a party to the substitution? She knew things might go wrong, so without telling Pattison she introduced the unknown woman into her place who, if things didn't go wrong, would be smuggled out and paid, if things went wrong would take the place of Mrs. O'Reilly, deceased.'

'But . . . but if you're going to argue like that, you're really naming Anne a murderer.'

Crane made no answer. Had they not appreciated the position they were both in, separately or collectively? Miles himself was not in the clear. What hard, provable facts the police had still pointed to his setting the fire as an act of revenge. Might he not have set it after making certain that Anne O'Reilly could not be burned to death in it...?

'Why can't you find the paintings?' demanded Miles.

Did he think the police hadn't tried? How many hours of work, by how many men, had been spent in searching for a clue to their whereabouts?

'You must at least have some idea what Reeves has done with them,' persisted Miles.

'We've a very good idea. Reeves is a professional and will have worked everything out professionally. To hide the five paintings in this country would be difficult and dangerous. If two layers of the crime were peeled back to make it clear that the paintings had been removed, then the insurance company would offer a reward for their safe return. Ten per cent of a million is a hundred thousand. There isn't a villain in the country who wouldn't sell his best oppo for that.

'So to be safe, the paintings went abroad. Where? When? Surely they went with Luque? If challenged by Customs at either end he would merely say they were copies, painted by him. A nice ironic touch: the false presented as genuine, the genuine as false. He took them to his home where he stored them, among other paintings of his own, then turned up in Madrid for the final payment due to him. That payment proved to be his death. Reeves then either collected the five paintings and took them away to another hiding place or, if he's as clever as I rate him, left them with Luque's family for a

small storage fee, certain they'd have no idea of wr
they really were.'

'If you can guess that much, you ought to be able to
trace out the paintings. Can't you make the Spanish police
co-operate ...'

Crane interrupted Miles. 'They couldn't have been
more helpful.'

'Then what's stopping them tracking down Luque's
home?'

'All his papers, including his identity card and passport,
were faked and investigations have failed to uncover a hint
of his real name.'

'Publicity ... ?'

'You're forgetting, he was engaged in forgery. His
family will not help to have his name and memory
smeared. In any case, Reeves will have made certain it's
worth their while not to talk.'

'There must be some way ...' began Miles desperately.

'If we knew within a small area – and I mean small –
where he lived, there would be: an intensive, blanket
search would almost certainly uncover his identity. But
we've no idea whereabouts in Spain he lived.'

'Photographs ...'

'His "accident" resulted in his face being far too badly
damaged for photos. The photograph in his faked passport
is, presumably by design, so poor that effective reproduc-
tion has been ruled right out.'

'But ... but then if you can't track down where he
lives, can't prove he handled the five stolen paintings ...
We ... Anne ...'

Crane looked unhappy

*   *   *   *   *

Miles poured out a third drink for himself. 'Why not have another?'

'No, thanks,' she answered dispiritedly.

'Anne, my darling, for God's sake remember that policemen have to be pessimists: if they start becoming cheerful, people think they aren't doing their job properly. It can't possibly be as bad as he tried to make out this morning.'

'Can't it?' she asked. 'If they never manage to prove the paintings were stolen, where are we?'

In the deep end, he thought. He drank. Was it really only days ago that he had told her he'd take her to Puerto de Tendraitx where they'd find the slice of Heaven he'd inadequately described?

'If the worst comes to the worst . . .' she began.

'The worst isn't going to happen,' he interrupted. He sat by her and put his arm tightly round her.

She spoke slowly and with hopeless regret. 'If only Luque had talked and told us about himself, then we might have learned something that would help say where he lived in Spain. But he was so bad tempered and his English so fractured . . .' She shrugged her shoulders.

He stroked her neck with the thumb of his left hand. He wanted to tell her that no matter what happened he would stand by her, but that would be to admit that the worst could happen and he'd just denied such possibility.

She spoke thoughtfully. 'All he ever said to me that I understood – or thought I did – was that every Christmas Eve he went to a monastery nearby where people from a long way came to hear the singing and how when there was snow it was so beautiful . . . Could that help us? Knowing he lived near a monastery?'

'It might do,' he answered, trying to sound hopeful. But how many monasteries were there in Spain?

182

'If Inspector Crane told the Spanish police . . .' He voice tailed away as she could no longer deny to herself the impossibility of such information being sufficient to identify Luque's home town. 'If only I'd listened to him more. For once, that day, he was in a talkative mood and a good temper. But I thought he must be slightly tight or making a pass at me, or both, and cut him short . . . If only I'd realized . . .'

None of them, he thought, from Pattison downwards, had realized the truth in time.

'He used to talk to Mrs. Barlowe much more, but that was mainly arguing. I think they really enjoyed disliking each other. I don't know what he thought she was, but she called him a cannibal. Wanting to eat all those awful dishes. She was so proud that she never cooked a single one of them. "As a decent, honest, God-fearing English-woman, with not a drop of foreign blood in me . . ." she used to say, hands on hips.' She managed a brief smile.

He remembered the day in the kitchen when Luque had come in and asked for some favourite dish because it would remind him of home. 'His horrible innards,' Mrs. Barlowe had said scornfully, conjuring up a wonderful picture . . . The name of the dish unexpectedly came back to him. Frito Mallorquin . . . Mallorquin . . . 'Anne!' he said excitedly.

'What on earth is it?'

'Luque didn't come from the Peninsula. He came from Mallorca.'

'How d'you know?'

He told her.

'Does that make a big difference?'

'Mallorca's only a fraction the size of Spain. And what's more . . .' He became silent.

'What's more what?'

'We know more than that he lived on the island. Because he talked to you about a monastery where people went at Christmas Eve to hear the singing and it was so beautiful when there was snow around . . . Only a few monasteries on the island will be noted for their singing to which the public go on Christmas Eve. And of those, even fewer will ever see snow. Snow in Mallorca's about as common as oases in the Sahara. The monastery has to be up in the mountains . . . With that sort of information, the police must be able to trace out where he lived. Crane said it would be possible if the area was very limited.'

'You really think so?'

'I know so.' He stood up. 'I must phone Crane and tell him. He's surely back in Ardscastle by now.'

He crossed to the telephone, which stood on a corner shelf, and dialled directory enquiries, who gave him the number of Ardscastle police station.

Crane was in and he listened without comment to what Miles told him. Then he asked Miles to repeat the evidence much more slowly – and calmly – while he took notes.

'They must be able to trace him now, mustn't they?' asked Miles.

'There's clearly a chance, but I must warn you . . .'

'Don't bother. I'll take your professional pessimism as read.'

There was a dry chuckle. 'Just trying to keep things within bounds, Mr. Miles. But if you insist, I'll become unprofessional enough to say that the odds look good from here.'

'Tell the Spaniards to take their fingers out.'

'I'll do what I can. Diplomatically.'

'And you'll let us know if . . .'

'Sooner than immediately.'

'If we remember anything fresh, we'll get right on to you. In the meantime . . . Thanks a lot for seeing so much of our side of things.'

'It's nice of you to say that. Just a moment, though, before you ring off. I wonder if you remember something I told you and have realized that one other aspect of the case could concern you quite considerably?'

Miles's voice expressed his sudden worry. 'What's that?'

'In a case like this one, the police always work to a certain degree with the insurance assessor and investigator. So when it became clear the paintings might have been stolen, not burned, I told them.'

'Well?'

'The insurance company has offered the usual reward for information leading to the recovery of the paintings.'

'You mean that we . . . ?'

'I mean that if the paintings are found because of what you've told me, that reward is very likely to be yours. So let's keep all our fingers and toes crossed . . . Good-bye.'

Miles slowly replaced the receiver.

'What did he say, Harry?' Anne asked. 'What did he tell you to make you look like that? Is it very bad?'

He shook his head. 'Just takes a bit of appreciating, that's all.' He briefly repeated what Crane had said.

'Harry — we could get enough money to escape for as long as we want?'

'That's right. Never-never land becoming ever-ever.'

'Oh, God! I think I'm going to cry.'

'And what could be a more feminine reaction than that?' he said, just before he kissed her.